To

George Dobbin

From
William Caldwell MacDonald

July 1945

M^CGOWAN CLIMBS A MOUNTAIN

McGowan Bales Out

(Chap. IX)

McGOWAN CLIMBS
A MOUNTAIN

BY

ALLAN ALDOUS

Illustrated by
MIGUEL MACKINLAY

OXFORD UNIVERSITY PRESS

LONDON　　　NEW YORK　　　TORONTO

First Published 1945

PRINTED IN GREAT BRITAIN BY
MORRISON AND GIBB LTD., LONDON AND EDINBURGH

CONTENTS

CHAPTER   PAGE

I. McGowan Smells a Story .   .   .   1

II. Good Practice   18

III. American Interlude .   .   .   33

IV. Sir Peter Gives Way   .   .   48

V. Under Way   62

VI. Onward and Upward   .   .   84

VII. Marooned   108

VIII. McGowan Takes to the Air   .   123

IX. The Summit   142

Envoi   163

CHAPTER I

McGOWAN SMELLS A STORY

GARRY McGOWAN sat back and relaxed as far as a French
railway compartment would permit him to relax. The
relaxing process was further complicated by his long legs,
which never seemed to find enough room to get comfortable. The train was crowded. Racks and corridors
were stacked with bulging rucksacks, many of which had
strapped to them climbing boots, ice-axes, and crampons
—the spiked frames that are strapped to the boots for
climbing on ice.

Sun-bronzed men and women who had packed their
brief winter sports holidays with as much excitement as
possible sat tiredly, their minds full of mingled memories
of wonderful experiences and the dismal prospect of the
dull office grind again in a few days' time.

Garry felt almost self-conscious in a belted tweed
overcoat and brown felt hat when nearly everyone else
was in ski suit or careless colourful sports clothes. He
himself had not had time for climbing or ski-ing ; he had
been covering the winter sports championships in Basle
and had been chained to his pen and notebook. Sports
reporting can sometimes be pretty exciting and sometimes
pretty dull. This assignment had been pretty dull
routine work.

He idly scanned the continental edition of the *Morning
Gazette*. There was his own report on yesterday's finals
on the sports page. A new comet had been discovered.
Someone had murdered someone. Someone in Parliament had raised the question of equal pay for men and
women. In America an expedition was being organized
to attack Kinchinga, a peak in the remote Himalayas,
and prove or disprove a Tibetan legend about a semi-
human monster that inhabited the mountain.

Garry couldn't be bothered ; he was tired. His hand

crushed the paper on his knees. The bare winter country-side flashed past the windows monotonously. Garry closed his eyes. The rhythm and clatter of the wheels rang in his ears.

From the opposite seat he heard voices. Two men who had entered the compartment carrying rucksacks with climbing boots slung on them were talking.

" What do you think of this Kinchinga business ? " asked one voice. " The experts say that peak's unclimbable."

" They've said that about lots of peaks—the Matterhorn, for example. But the Matterhorn was climbed eventually. The funny thing, though, is that there's an English party planning to attempt Kinchinga too."

Garry opened one eye. A British and an American expedition in a race to the summit of the mighty Kinchinga had the odour of big news.

The man speaking was young and lean and as brown as leather. The other said : " I've heard nothing about it."

" You wouldn't. It's Sir Peter Rawson's show and he feels pretty strongly about publicity. Mention newspapers and he shuts up in his shell like a clam."

" Then how is it that you know about it ? "

" My uncle is one of the proposed party. He and Sir Peter have climbed together for years. I tried to persuade him to let me in on the party, but it's no go. I've got to be a good boy and finish my law course."

" I'd give anything to be in on a show like that," said the other.

Garry opened his other eye.

" I say," he said. " Pardon my butting in. I know it's quite inexcusable, but I couldn't help overhearing what you just said. Who did you say was planning that expedition to Kinchinga ? "

" Sorry," said the very brown young man. " That wasn't supposed to be overheard."

" Then I'm rebuffed," sighed Garry. " I guess it is a cheek slamming over a question like that right in the middle of a private conversation. But, as I said, I couldn't help overhearing and I have a most impetuous curiosity. It's always getting me into hot water. Please accept my apology."

" Sure," said the young man. " I often overhear remarks myself and find myself just dying to chip in. But I'm afraid I haven't got the nerve."

" In the newspaper game," Garry explained, " you've just got to have nerve. I've developed a hide that bullets would bounce off."

The other two laughed.

" Then you're a reporter ? " asked one.

" Guilty," admitted Garry. " My name is Garry McGowan."

" So you're the famous Garry McGowan," said the man with the mountaineering uncle. " I'm very glad to meet you. I follow your column in the *Gazette* and I think it's grand. It's a lot more than mere reporting."

" I try to make it so," Garry told him.

" You succeed all right," said the other man.

" Well, we may as well introduce ourselves," said the very brown one. " This is Johnny Pascoe and I'm Colin Meighan."

" I'm glad to meet you," said Garry. " I observe you're both climbers."

" Every chance we get," said Colin.

" The trouble is we get so little time," Johnny complained. " Stuck to an office chair most of the year. I often wish I'd taken up journalism. You do get around a bit in that game."

" You get around all right," Garry conceded. " But you get precious little time for yourself. One moment you may be chasing a story in Little Stick-in-the-Mud and an hour later you may be on your way to Timbuctoo."

They talked about their interests and their ambitions, and before many miles had slipped past were as intimate as old friends.

At last Garry said : " Look, I'm sorry to bring the subject up again. But if British and American expeditions are going to race to the summit of Kinchinga it spells news that makes my fingers itch for a typewriter. Be a sport and spill the beans."

Colin grinned. " O.K.," he said. " But this is off the record. And if you do print it, it won't do you any good anyway, because Sir Peter will only write to the editor saying it's an idle rumour, that there's not an atom of truth in it, and demanding a withdrawal. A couple of local reporters did get wind of the expedition three or four months ago and printed something about it. He did that to them."

" But why ? " Garry demanded.

" I don't know," shrugged Colin. " Except that he says publicity is vulgar, and he detests it. He climbs mountains for his own pleasure and it's got nothing at all to do with anyone else in the world. That's what he says."

" Well, I suppose he's got a right to feel what he likes about it," said Garry. " Still, I don't easily let up on a good story. What is the name ? "

" O.K., then. He's Sir Peter Rawson," answered Colin. " You'll find him at 59 Kingston Crescent, Kensington."

Garry made a note of it. " Thanks a lot," he said.

Colin grinned. " For heaven's sake don't let on where you learned about the stunt. But really, you're wasting your time. In the first place he won't see you, and in the second place, even if he does see you, you won't get anything out of him."

Garry smiled quietly. " We'll see. I think I heard you mention a while back something about unclimbable mountains that were climbed after all," he said pointedly.

A few hours later Garry burst into the office of Greg Carmody, sports editor of the *Gazette*. Carmody was poring over some proofs, a cigarette dangling from a corner of his mouth.

" Why don't you knock before you enter ? " shouted Carmody without looking up.

" Climb down off the high horse, Greg," said Garry.

Carmody glanced up sharply through his horn-rims.

" Oh, it's you," he grunted, calming down not a little. " Wondered when you'd get back. I've got a job for you." Then as an afterthought he added : " By the way, nice bit of work that winter sports series. Have a cigar."

" Thanks, Greg," said Garry. " But one of these days you'll get it into that muddled skull of yours that I don't smoke cigars or anything else."

" No, no, of course not. I remember now."

" I can't afford to," explained Garry.

" Eh ? Can't afford to ? You're one of the best-paid newspaper men in London."

Garry grinned. " You've got me wrong," he said. " The way you send me scuttling here, there, and every-where I'd crack up in no time if I didn't keep absolutely sound in wind and limb. And smoking doesn't do the old wheeze-box a lot of good."

" Stop preaching," shouted Carmody irritably. He himself had never been seen by anyone without a cigarette in his mouth. It was even rumoured that he had cigarettes of immense length specially made which he lighted each night and smoked by means of a long rubber tube while he slept. But that rumour had never been confirmed. " I said I had a job for you," he went on. " I want——"

Garry cut him short. " That's nothing new. And I've got something to break to you, too."

" Who's chief around here ? " demanded Carmody, thumping his desk. " You listen to me first."

Garry out-shouted him. " No. You're going to listen to me first. I smell a story that will run all the way from the sports column to the front page."

Carmody growled like a dog with a bone. He loved to bark and shout and make a lot of noise, but his bark was quite harmless. It was when he was very quiet and puffed very hard at his cigarette that there was trouble in the air.

" Listen," said Garry. " This is the biggest mountain-eering story since the Matterhorn was conquered. Did you see that an American expedition is preparing to have a crack at Kinchinga ? "

Carmody grunted an affirmative.

" Well, I've just learned that a British party has also been planning for a long time to do the same thing. Think of it ! An Anglo-American race to the summit of Kinchinga ! Boy, it's immense ! "

Carmody rose to his feet, his eyes glittering.

" Is that true ? " he demanded.

" It sure is."

" When does it come off ? "

" That's what I've got to find out."

" Holy kippers ! " Carmody murmured to himself. " What a story ! "

" But there's a snag," Garry continued. " Sir Peter Rawson is organizing the expedition, and I gather he's got a bee in his bonnet about publicity. He just doesn't want to have anything to do with newspapers."

" The devil he doesn't ! " snapped Carmody. " I know that, laddie. He's done some of the finest ascents of modern times in the Dolomites and the Urals. First-rate stories all of them, and the reporter who could get a single one out of him just doesn't exist."

" I'm going to get one," Garry asserted.

" Don't waste your time."

There was a knock on the door.

" Keep out," roared Carmody. " I'm busy."

The door opened and Jimmy, the copy boy, came in with a batch of proofs. He always received that response to his knock on the door. He no longer took any notice of it.

" Hullo, Mr. McGowan," he said.

" Hullo, Jimmy," said Garry. " How's the football ? "

" Fine. We won on Sat'day. And I'm captain now."

" Congrats, old fellow. I must come and write you up some time."

" You're kidding, Mr. McGowan."

" Maybe I'm not, Jimmy," Garry said, pursing his lips thoughtfully.

" Gee ! " gasped Jimmy, breathless at the thought. " I liked your winter sports stories."

" I'm glad you did."

" They made me wish I had tons of money to go ski-ing and tobogganing on one of those big slides and things."

" You don't have to have tons of money to enjoy life, you know, Jimmy."

" Or I'd like to be a sports writer like you and travel all over the world. Where are you going next ? "

" I'm not sure. But I think it may be the Himalayas." Carmody found his voice at last.

" It will be nothing of the sort. It will be America," he snapped. " Go on, clear out, boy. Football on the Common indeed, when we're talking business ! Go on, clear out, you lazy young . . ." He spluttered into silence.

" I'll see you later, Jimmy," Garry said.

Jimmy went out and closed the door.

" And now," demanded Garry. " Why am I going to America ? "

" Because Mayfield in New York has gone and caught appendicitis and left us uncovered for the middle-weight championship fight. You fly over in the Clipper on Monday."

" Thanks. You never give me much chance to grow roots, do you, Greg ? "

" You like it that way and don't pretend you don't," said Carmody, suddenly melting into a chuckle.

" Well, maybe I do," said Garry.

" Now, just you lay off over the week-end and build up your strength." He slapped Garry's broad shoulders and permitted himself a ghost of a smile.

Garry went into his own untidy office. He slung his hat into a corner, scattered a pile of reference books, proofs, and miscellaneous papers into even worse confusion, and at last unearthed a telephone directory. He thumbed down the R's. He frowned as he committed a number to memory. Then he picked up the telephone.

" Hullo, get me Kensington one-oh-one-two, please," he said. " Hullo, Kensington one-oh-one-two ? Could I speak to Sir Peter Rawson, please ? "

In the receiver a precise, somewhat affected man's voice said : " This is Sir Peter's secretary. Who shall I say, please ? "

" It doesn't matter about the name. He won't recognize it anyway."

" I'm afraid Sir Peter will not take a call from any unknown person. He is very strict in that respect. He only accepts calls from persons known to him."

" This is important," bluffed Garry.

" I'm sorry, sir," said the voice. " Sir Peter's instructions are inflexible. If, however, you care to give me your name and the nature of your business I shall convey them to him and he will communicate with you at his pleasure."

" It doesn't matter, thanks," Garry muttered and hung up.

Garry scratched his chin thoughtfully. So that was how the land lay. It was obvious that Sir Peter could be approached by little less than breaking and entering. Garry sat in his chair and tilted it back, his feet on the desk. He tapped his temples as though trying to rouse a solution to the problem.

At last he rose and went from the quiet of his office to the composing-room, alive with hurrying, aproned, inky men and the groan and clatter of the battery of linotype machines. He found Jimmy waiting for proofs from a galley of newly-set type.

" Jimmy," he said, " you fancy yourself as a footballer, don't you ? "

" Well," replied Jimmy modestly and reddening a little, " I wouldn't get me game with Chelsea exactly, if you know what I mean—not yet, that is. But I'm not too bad, else I wouldn't be captain of our team."

" Of course not," agreed Garry. " You're pretty accurate when you kick a ball, I suppose ? "

" Well, I've snapped some pretty useful goals in my

time. If there's a hole there I'll put the ball through it nine times out of ten."

"Then maybe you will play for Chelsea one of these days," Garry suggested.

"Gosh, I'd give anything for that. I've still got a few years to go, of course."

"Of course. Now, Jimmy, how would you like me to write up one of your matches?"

"You said that before, Mr. McGowan. You're kidding."

"No, Jimmy, I'm not kidding."

"But no one else has heard of us except the kids in our district. That isn't news."

"Jimmy, you read my column, don't you?"

"Every day, Mr. McGowan."

"Then you know that so far as I'm concerned it's the good, clean game that matters. A good hard contest between fifth-raters who put their heart and soul into it and play for the game's sake means more to me than all the commercial games in the world where the players win or lose according to how much money goes into their pockets. I could write you up, Jimmy, and make the public like it."

"I don't know what to say, Mr. McGowan. The fellers'll be crazy when I tell 'em."

"Good. I'll write you up. But you've got to do something for me in return."

"Anything you like, Mr. McGowan."

"You live in South Kensington, don't you? And I expect you carry your football through the streets when you go to the ground?"

"Yes."

"And sometimes you boot the leather in the street if the coast is clear of coppers?"

"Aw, maybe we do sometimes," Jimmy owned up uncomfortably.

"Jimmy, you said a moment ago you were a pretty hot shot."

"Well, I'm not too bad."

" Good. Do you think you could kick a football through a window, for instance ? "

" I reckon I could."

" Fine.   To-morrow I want you to come along with me and kick your football through a window."

Horror showed in Jimmy's face and his mouth gaped. " But, Mr. McGowan," he protested, " do you mean an open or closed one ? "

" A closed one. I want it to be a lovely shattering crash."

" But the coppers——"

" Now, don't worry, Jimmy, I'll see you through."

" But——"

" Do you want that write-up—or no ? "

Jimmy gulped hard and nodded.

" Now this is what I want you to do. . . ."

Garry outlined his plans.

The following afternoon Garry stood by a corner commanding a view up Kingston Crescent. At the other end of the crescent a couple of youths aged about fourteen, one with a football under his arm, strolled nonchalantly along, whistling to themselves. One youth looked around guiltily. The street was deserted. He dropped the ball and began dribbling it along, passing it to the other. They passed it to each other from opposite sides of the street as they worked along. After some distance one of them became obviously more intent on his business. His eyes flashed towards a big white house, shrewdly judging the range. Then came the hollow thump of a ball being kicked hard. The sphere sailed up towards the white house. There was a resounding crash and the tinkle of falling glass. All along the street windows shot up and heads popped out.

The youths fled down the crescent as though the whole police force were on their heels. Garry stepped out and grabbed one. The other avoided him and disappeared round the corner. A few people had begun to gather.

" You let me go, mister," pleaded the youth Garry had

captured. Under a drooping lock of his tousled hair one eye blinked—or maybe winked.

" Oh no," said Garry sternly, surreptitiously returning the wink. " What's the game, eh ? When I hear a crash and see someone in such a hurry as you were I know he's up to no good. You come along with me."

" Garn, let the kid go," said a passer-by. " Weren't y'ever young yerself ? "

" Yes," snapped Garry. " And not so long ago either. But you mind your own business, see."

Garry was an inch and a half over six feet and turned the scale to thirteen and a half stone. The passer-by deemed discretion the better part of valour, and with a scowl went on his way. Garry hauled Jimmy away towards the big white house. Its front door was now wide open. A gaping maid stood there. On the footpath was a dapper little man with sleek, oiled black hair and a trim black moustache.

" This is one of the culprits," said Garry. " The other got away. What has he been up to ? "

" They kicked a football through Sir Peter's window."

" Oh, is that all," said Garry. " I thought it was something serious."

" Isn't that serious enough ? " snapped the man. " Young hooligans ! They must be taught a lesson. I'll phone for the police."

The voice was the one Garry had heard on the telephone the day before, the voice of Sir Peter's secretary.

" I agree they must be taught a lesson," said Garry. " But don't you think calling the police a little too drastic ? He doesn't look a young scoundrel exactly. I think a good talking-to would meet the case."

" Perhaps you're right," said the little man. " I'll ask Sir Peter to deal with him."

He prepared to return inside the house.

" I say," called Garry. " I can't stand here in the street all day holding the lad."

" Then perhaps you'd better bring him inside."

Garry pushed Jimmy up the steps. The maid closed

2

the big door behind them when they entered. Garry winked at Jimmy again as they stood in the lofty well-furnished hall and watched the secretary hurrying fussily up a wide oak staircase and out of sight.

" It's working so far," he said.

On the walls were paintings of mountains, photographs of climbing parties and men clinging to rocks above breath-taking precipices. Garry moved about studying them. A few minutes later the secretary returned, followed by a tall man with a lithe, springy figure. His face was thin, well-formed, and tanned. Only his receding hair, greying slightly, suggested that he must be in his forties.

" This is Sir Peter Rawson," announced the secretary.

" Good afternoon, sir," said Garry.

" Good afternoon," returned Sir Peter. " Now what is all the bother ? "

" I was walking along Parker Street," explained Garry, struggling hard to make his white lie sound like the truth, " when I heard a crash of breaking glass and saw two youngsters streaking down Kingston Crescent. I collared one and brought him along. I didn't know what he had been up to till I learned that he had put a football through one of your windows. Your . . . er . . ." He nodded towards the secretary.

" My secretary," confirmed Sir Peter.

" Your secretary wished to call the police, but I thought that a little drastic."

" I see," said Sir Peter. He approached Jimmy. " Well, young man, what have you got to say for yourself ? "

" My mate and me, we was booting the ball along the street and I slipped and accidentally kicked the ball extra hard and it shot straight up through your window. I'm sorry, sir."

" I see. You know you're not supposed to play football in the streets ? "

" Yes, sir. I'll pay, sir."

" Why did you run away ? " Garry chipped in.

" I was scared of the coppers."

" It wasn't very brave, was it ? If you find yourself in trouble you should stand up and face it, not run away from it."

" Yes, sir."

" The gentleman is quite right," said Sir Peter. " You understand that ? "

" Yes, sir."

" All right, you've had a bad scare. I don't think you'll play footer in the street again in a hurry. And you can forget about paying this time. Clarke, show this youth out through the back entrance. . . . Oh, and you can return his ball to him."

The secretary escorted Jimmy away.

" That was very generous, sir," said Garry.

" Not at all. I once put a cricket ball through a window as a youngster and cut and ran. I got away with it. But I lived in an agony of apprehension for weeks after lest the guilt be traced to me. I decided then never to run away from trouble again. And I never have."

" I understand the feeling," said Garry. " By the way, sir, this is an extraordinary coincidence. I was actually walking along this way to see you when this incident happened. I was amazed when your secretary announced Sir Peter Rawson."

" And what were you coming to see me about ? "

" I'm a newspaper man."

" Indeed," said Sir Peter crisply. " Had it not been for this—er—incident you most assuredly would not have seen me."

" Then I suppose the sporting thing to do is not to take unfair advantage of a mere accident," Garry suggested, not without a certain cunning. He had weighed up Sir Peter pretty shrewdly. " Good afternoon, sir." He moved towards the door.

" Just a moment," Sir Peter called. " Don't tell me I'm dreaming, or are you really a news-hound with a conscience ? "

" Well, sir, you've got to forget about conscience quite a lot in the newspaper racket. But I believe in playing the game. I'm Garry McGowan."

" Garry McGowan ! " exclaimed Sir Peter. He advanced and shook Garry's hand. " I'm glad to meet you, McGowan. I admire your work very much indeed. I consider sport one of the finest aspects of English life, and I am indeed glad of the stand you take against commercial interests which are destroying all that is fine in our sport."

Garry was overwhelmed with surprise.

" You know, sir, I didn't quite know what to expect. But I did think from what I'd heard that you must be a bit of a dragon."

" Good heavens, no," laughed Sir Peter. " I'm a very quiet, ordinary person. And it's because I want to go on being a quiet, ordinary person that I dislike any sort of publicity. What did you want to see me about, anyway ? "

" I heard a whisper that you were organizing an expedition to Kinchinga."

" And how did you come to hear it, may I ask ? "

" I overheard a chance conversation arising out of the announcement of an American expedition. I foresaw big news. What about it, sir ? "

" Nothing doing, McGowan. Much as I admire your work, I should never have granted you an interview."

" But I don't understand, sir," protested Garry.

" One of the worst diseases of the modern world is publicity fever. I detest publicity. If a man wants to get himself in the news, or is indifferent as to whether he gets his name in print or not, well and good. But I maintain the right of the individual to do as he likes without having the rest of the world gassing about him. I climb mountains because I love the mountains and the sport. I seek neither fame nor money. I want to climb simply because I like climbing, and it has nothing whatever to do with the rest of the world."

" I can understand that to a certain extent," Garry conceded. " But at the same time great feats of skill and endurance can be more than just a sensational bit of news. They can inspire people. Britishers take a pride in being British. They like to read about British successes, and they're better Britishers for having that pride. Now that this American expedition is being planned you could do a great bit of patriotic work. A race between the two countries to the summit of Kinchinga would be wonderful. Think of the clean, healthy rivalry of the thing. Two continents would go crazy over it, and it would be a tremendous fillip to the feeling between the two countries."

" McGowan, you're wasting good breath," said Sir Peter. " And you don't even know that I'm going to Kinchinga."

" But you are, aren't you, sir ? " Garry asked eagerly.

" Listen, McGowan. I like you. I like your writing, your stand for clean honest-to-God playing of the game. Now I've met you in person you strike me as being sincere and honest in yourself. What I'm going——"

" Just a moment, Sir Peter," Garry interposed. " Before you get any further with this McGowan-boosting line there's something I've got to get off my chest. You're making me feel pretty cheap because I do stoop to tricks sometimes. That football through your window was no accident. I honestly meant to come clean about it anyway sooner or later. But I just had to see you, and it was the only way I could think up."

" Do you know, McGowan, I half suspected that. And I like you for—er—coming clean, as you call it."

" Well, that makes me feel better," said Garry, breathing more easily. " Sir Peter, you're what they call a swell guy over in the States."

" Then I think we understand each other, McGowan. We can talk. But I want you to understand we are talking as man to man. You can forget you're a journalist. I'm pretty good at judging character, and I don't think I'm wrong about you. You wouldn't betray a confidence."

" I wouldn't be where I am now, sir, if I did," Garry

told him. " A good story means an awful lot to me, but a good name means even more."

" Good," said Sir Peter. " Well, as a matter of fact I am making an attack on Kinchinga. I've gathered all possible data about the mountain, organized transport and supplies, and the whole business is almost completed. I anticipate sailing for India in about a month's time. As no doubt you've gathered, I'm a wealthy man, and this expedition is entirely my own responsibility. For years I've thought and planned of an expedition to Kinchinga, and at last it's almost a fact. I'm doing it for one reason only. I want to reach the summit of that mountain on my own two legs. My reward will be to stand there with no higher land around me. I ask no more."

" But being first to climb the mountain . . ."

" There is a certain satisfaction in being there first, but that does not worry me. I shall carry on as though the American expedition did not exist."

" You're not stirred by the prospect of a contest—a race ? "

" That urge is something I have to sit on. Mountaineering is a matter of patience, of planning, of pitting your wits against the forces of Nature—and, of course, gravitation."

Garry grinned.

" To allow oneself to get excited," Sir Peter continued, " to take chances for the sake of speed, is courting disaster."

" What about this legend of a monster ? " Garry asked. " Do you hope to solve that mystery ? "

" A monster does not enter into the project. Pretty well every peak in the Himalayas has got some monster or god inhabiting it. They're just the talk of simple, superstitious natives. The newspapers have given the story ridiculous publicity for the sake of sensation."

" Look, sir, I do wish you would let me write about your project."

" And be pestered by every crank and newspaper man

in London ? " grunted Sir Peter. " No, thank you.
This expedition is quite, quite private ; trespassers will
be kicked out in double-quick time."

" Your mind is quite made up ? "

" Absolutely. My friends will tell you that I'm a man
of strong and fixed opinions, and that I'm absolutely
inflexible."

Garry knew he meant it. He was a little depressed
that the interview had borne very little fruit after all.
" Well, I guess there's nothing else to do except say good-
day. And thanks for being a sportsman."

" I'm glad I met you, McGowan. By the way, have
you ever done any climbing ? "

" Nothing exciting. One or two of the conventional
peaks in the Bernese Alps accompanied by some guides
whose only idea was to get me up and down again in the
shortest possible time for the longest possible fee."

Sir Peter laughed. " That's scarcely what we call
mountaineering. Look, McGowan, three of us are going
to North Wales over the week-end to do a bit of training
work. We'll be on rock courses mostly. Would you care
to join us ? It will give you an idea of what real mountaineering can be like."

Garry brightened up. " By jove, that sounds great !
Sure, count me in."

Garry ran straight into Carmody when he returned to
the office.

" What the devil do you mean by running away with
my copy boy ? " Carmody demanded, the few hairs
remaining on his head seeming to bristle with rage.

" I borrowed him in a very good cause," Garry
laughed. " I'll tell you about it some day if you're
good."

He pushed past Carmody, leaving him spluttering
with wrath. He sought out Jimmy, now back on the
job.

" Hullo, Mr. McGowan," Jimmy greeted him. " Did
it work ? "

" Yes and no, Jimmy. Sir Peter's a human oyster, but

I've got a hunch I'll be going to India to cover a big story before very long."

"How did I do?" asked Jimmy.

"Fine. If you weren't going to be a footballer I'd suggest you go on the films."

"Old Carmody didn't half carry on when I got back. If he'd had any hair to spare he'd have torn it all out. Coo, what a temper!"

"Don't you worry about him. He'll get over it."

"You won't forget our write-up?" asked Jimmy anxiously.

"Don't you worry about that either. I'll do it just as soon as I can. I'm going right off to North Wales now. On Monday I go to New York. I'll see if I can fit it in when I get back. In the meantime—how is the football club's funds?"

"Pretty unhealthy," answered Jimmy.

"Perhaps this will warm them up," suggested Garry, and pressed a couple of notes into his hand. Jimmy stared at them incredulously.

CHAPTER II

GOOD PRACTICE

GARRY took a taxi to his rooms in Baker Street. He never knew quite why he retained them, except that it was nice to know you had some place you could call your own, some place where you could dump your books and pictures and knick-knacks, even if you hardly ever set foot in the place because you were streaking about all over the world. Now he dug out some old slacks, a wind-cheater jacket, a sweater, sports shirt, underclothes, and from the bottom of a pile of miscellanea in a cupboard he unearthed his old nailed climbing boots. They were board-hard and badly in need of dubbining. He squeezed all the kit into his rucksack, sailed down the stairs, hailed a taxi and was whisked to Paddington Station.

It was early the following morning that he arrived at Corwen. He took a car to Capel Curig, where, at one of the little hotels commanding glorious views of snow-capped Snowdonia, he was to meet Sir Peter and his companions.

Sir Peter and his friends arrived about 10 a.m., having flown down in Sir Peter's own plane. In the lounge of the hotel Garry met Hastings Bourne and Dr. Eric Dodd, both well-known climbers. They were a little younger than Sir Peter. When Sir Peter in introducing them mentioned the name Garry McGowan, they both looked at him incredulously. Sir Peter laughed.

" It's all right, boys, McGowan is here as a man, not a reporter."

Garry grinned wryly. " It sounds as though a reporter is not quite human," he commented. " Well, maybe you're right."

The others laughed. Over lunch they discussed plans for the morrow's climbing.

" There's plenty of snow about," Sir Peter said. " So much the better. It will more closely approximate to the conditions we'll meet on Kinchinga. Rock work in such weather is going to be tough work indeed."

" Look here," said Garry, " I'm not an expert, you know. I feel I'll be something of a drag."

" You don't want to worry about that," said Bourne, a big, cheerful fellow who looked as though he could crush rocks in his huge hands. " I've heard of some of your exploits. I'd say you had your fair share of nerve and toughness. Just leave the rest to us. We'll find it good practice, anyway. We'll have to nurse native porters over tricky places when we really get going."

" I wish I were in on that expedition," Garry said wistfully.

" You mean writing about it ? " asked Dr. Dodd, a small, dark, wiry man.

" I didn't have that in mind just then," Garry explained. " What I meant was it would be a wonderful experience."

" I'm afraid it's quite impossible," said Sir Peter. " In

an expedition of such magnitude you've got to choose your men carefully. Each man must be a specialist in his own way and we must work together as a team. It's experience that counts."

"I quite realize that," said Garry. "But I wouldn't mind going only as far as the base camp and covering the story."

"There is no story," Sir Peter reaffirmed.

"I know," grinned Garry ruefully. "I was just indulging in a little wishful thinking. All the same, I think this secrecy can be carried too far. Once you get on the trail surely it would do no harm to let the world know. No one could pester you then."

"They could when we returned," Sir Peter reminded him.

"Maybe," agreed Garry. "But you'll get that in any case—only probably worse. Because a big expedition can't assemble and move into the mountains without anyone knowing it. The newspapers would tell the world that an expedition was going into the Himalayas even if they didn't know where it was striking for. The curiosity of the world would be aroused and you'd suffer more from fool questions when you got back than if you made known your plans through the press."

"There's something in what McGowan says," commented Bourne.

"I'm not to be persuaded," asserted Sir Peter. "I will not pander to a sensation press and mere vulgar curiosity."

"What do you fellows think?" demanded Garry of the others.

"It's nothing to do with us," said Dr. Dodd. "We abide by Sir Peter's decisions."

"Anyway, this is an exploit Britain might very well be proud of. If Britain is proud of it then surely there's no harm in your being proud of it," pursued Garry. "I guess you've got nothing to be ashamed of, Sir Peter."

"I'm sure you would grow quite eloquent if I allowed you to proceed, McGowan. But the oratory even of a

Churchill would not change my attitude. Shall we drop the subject ? "

Garry was abashed. " Sorry," he mumbled. " I'm afraid I carry myself away. It's one of my failings. I promise I'll be good."

They laughed at his assumed expression of youthful remorse.

Early the following day the party, clad in wind-cheaters, carrying rucksacks and girded with ropes, strode down the road towards the Nant-Ffrancon Pass. After a six-mile tramp they left the road and struck up the rough, steep turf towards the Carnedds. Behind them the sharp, dark, prickly cone of Y Tryfaen soared upwards and lost its head in the clouds.

After a couple of hours the cloud drifted away, revealing the white-capped peaks in magnificent array. These mountains were babies—just clearing the three-thousand-foot mark. The giant Kinchinga touched 23,680 feet. Such immensity of rock and snow and ice was inconceivable. The three men who accompanied Garry were going to assail its tremendous bulk. They would climb as they climbed here in North Wales. The technique would be the same. But with what other differences ! Kinchinga would be no one-day's tramping and climbing. It would mean weeks of working through tropical jungle and uncharted country. As they reached higher altitudes the rarefied air would torture their lungs and steal the strength from their limbs. Perfect climbing technique would be taken for granted then. It would be physical endurance that counted. And in the last stages it would be sheer will-power, when gasping lungs and leaden limbs cried out to quit.

The party trudged up the comparatively easy slopes and were soon in snow. They crossed the hump of a saddle that linked Pen Helig, a spur of the Carnedd range, with Carnedd Llewellyn itself. They dropped swiftly on the far side, glissading down the steep slopes of a gully. The snow spurted and swished as their boots slithered through it. They balanced themselves with the help of their ice-axes on that exhilarating chute. When they reached the bottom they worked round until they were under the towering black cliffs of Pen Helig.

Sir Peter called a halt for refreshment. This would be the starting-point for a stiff rock climb. Garry looked upwards. The almost perpendicular mass of rock seemed about as climbable as the outside of a New York sky-scraper. The whole cliff seemed about to topple over and crush them, an illusion created by the cloud drifting over its bluff.

After hot coffee and sandwiches the party roped up. Sir Peter led. Garry was third, between Bourne and Dr. Dodd. The climb was an education for Garry. He marvelled at the sure, methodical, graceful, seemingly leisurely movements of the older men. They explained their methods as they went along, showing Garry where the holds were, and how to take advantage of them.

Garry was a natural athlete, and he fell fairly easily into their methods. But only years of experience could give him their rhythmic, assured movement. The climbers moved one at a time, the others keeping the rope tension right—not too taut, not too loose. As each moved the others braced themselves to take the shock should the moving man make a false move and fall.

After half an hour of delicate climbing, calling for careful well-balanced movements, the party had achieved several hundred feet of height. Garry looked down.

" Gosh, now I know how a fly must feel walking up a wall. It's just as well heights don't make me giddy."

At length they reached a small flat slab of rock—a sort of platform—where they decided to rest. It was exhilarating to look across that deep valley from the security of the ledge. Sir Peter's eyes constantly scanned the rock above him, sorting out a route that would " go."

After a breather, Sir Peter pushed on. It would be the last pitch. Another thirty feet and they would be safe on the flat top of the spur. But those thirty feet were very tricky indeed. Sir Peter's smooth, flexible movements carried him via tiny foot- and hand-holds to a position about fifteen feet higher. He was motionless for some time.

" This is pretty tough," he called down. " I'm afraid it won't go."

The others watched him as he stood delicately balanced on a tiny ledge while one hand groped upwards for another hold. There was a horizontal crack but he could not reach it. He retraced his steps with slow caution and then struck away in another direction. Again he drew blank. He tried in a third direction and manœuvred round an exposed, projecting bluff. As he worked round by scarcely workable hand- and foot-holds, Garry was aware of his heart beating uncomfortably fast. Beneath Sir Peter was a sheer drop of six hundred feet. Sir Peter disappeared from view. Inch by inch the safety rope edged across the bluff, paid out by Bourne.

At last they heard Sir Peter's voice.

" This looks as if it will go. I've got a good broad stand here, and I've got the rope belayed to a spike of rock. Work around, Bourne."

Bourne set out on the hazardous traverse. He was a big, heavy man. Garry sat on the snowy ledge, his legs stiffly braced, his heels firm against a projecting ridge of rock. He passed the rope round his back and over one shoulder towards Bourne. If Bourne slipped, the friction of the rope on Garry's back would enable him to hold the weight.

Slowly Bourne moved round the bluff, releasing but one hand- or foot-hold at a time. Then with shocking suddenness a piece of rock snapped away with a report like a pistol-shot. Bourne's leg shot into space. Garry's heart leapt wildly. For a moment Bourne's hands scrabbled on the rock face. Then he slipped into space. Garry tautened every muscle in his body. He winced as the rope cut sickeningly into his back. A grunt of pain came from Bourne as he swung inwards and crashed heavily against the rock. Garry gasped with the torture of the cutting rope, but he retained his grip and Bourne swung gently in space—held.

Sir Peter's voice shouted urgently from round the corner, " Is he all right ? "

" I think so," Dr. Dodd shouted back.

" I can't hold him all day," groaned Garry.

Dodd quickly unroped himself, and taking the line from Garry, hitched it as tightly as possible to a small spur of rock. Then he eased the rope across Garry's shoulder until Bourne's weight was taken by the spur on his side and Sir Peter's belay on the other side of the bluff.

Bourne was moaning softly, his face ashen.

" Are you hurt ? " Dodd called.

" It's my leg," grunted Bourne, in obvious pain.

Garry quickly loosened his burning muscles and again seated himself with his feet braced against the ridge. He seized the rope with both hands, bent his legs, and then powerfully drove them straight, his seat sliding back through the snow. It was the drive that had helped propel many an eights crew to victory. Behind him Dodd took a purchase on the spur of rock while Garry got a fresh grip. It was agonizing work. Despite the cold Garry sweated exceedingly. Gradually Bourne was drawn closer to the safety of the ledge. At last Garry could seize his arm. Dodd secured his last purchase with a hitch and came to Garry's assistance. Between them they hauled Bourne on to the ledge.

" We've got him safe," shouted Garry.

" Thank God," came back Sir Peter's voice, full of fervent relief.

Dr. Dodd quickly examined Bourne.

" It's my leg," groaned Bourne. " Gave it a deuce of a crack."

The doctor examined the leg with expert speed.

" Broken tibia," he announced grimly, and shouted the information again for the benefit of Sir Peter.

They were in a very grim situation. The winter day was short. There were only about three hours of light

GRADUALLY BOURNE WAS DRAWN CLOSER TO THE SAFETY OF THE LEDGE.

remaining. Four men on an exposed mountain face, one of them with a broken leg. Dr. Dodd cut some rope into lengths and lashed Bourne's legs together, thus making the sound one a splint for the injured.

" You'd better try to get back here, Peter," the doctor shouted.

Garry manned the safety rope and drew it slowly towards him. Sir Peter's progress was painfully slow ; for a long time he was stationary.

" It's hopeless," he called at last. " The rock that broke away under Bourne's weight was the only possible workable hold here. I'll try to make the top and go for help. I'm afraid it's impossible to get him down the way we came up. We'd never make it before dark, and in any case the poor fellow would suffer torture every time we moved him."

" Right," Dr. Dodd shouted back. They heard the scraping of Sir Peter's iron-shod boots fading away.

" This is a nasty position," murmured Dodd, shaking his head gravely. " Maybe we're tough enough to survive a night on the ledge even in this weather. But poor Bourne is suffering pretty badly from shock. He needs immediate warmth and comfort. He would never survive the night. I doubt whether Peter could get to the road and find help and get back here before dark even if he did find a quick route to the top."

Garry looked at the injured man. His eyes were closed and his breathing was slow and noisy. He moaned occasionally. His face had a nasty pallor. Dr. Dodd poured coffee from the thermos for him. Garry looked up the rock face desperately, seeking some route up that formidable, beetling black wall. It was hopeless. How could he hope to succeed where Sir Peter had failed ?

In the silence they again heard the scrabbling of metal-shod boots. Then came Sir Peter's voice : " I say, you fellows, it's no go. Not an earthly chance this way. I'm stuck here too."

Garry bit his lip as he looked down again at Bourne. Once more he scanned the rock face, slowly tracing every inch. About twenty feet above him a rock projected like a cannon from a fortress. If he could get to that rock the rest would probably be fairly easy. A desperate scheme formed in his mind. It was a barely possible chance.

" I'm going to try something," he shouted to Sir Peter.

" There isn't a way up there either," Sir Peter called back. " You'll kill yourself if you try."

" I'm not going to try—at least, not the way you think. But there's another possible chance. When I was covering a rodeo in Texas once, Billy Theodore, the Lower West rope champion, taught me to throw a lariat. There's a projecting rock up there. If I can make it we're half-way home."

" You can't swing a rope on this ledge," protested Dr. Dodd. " It's much too narrow."

" I know," Garry agreed. " I've got to get out where I've got throwing room."

" How ? "

" I'll show you."

He took the slack of the rope they had used to haul Bourne to safety. One end was still hitched to the spur of rock on the left-hand side of the ledge. Garry measured the distance with his eye, then fastened the rope about his chest under the armpits.

" Now get a purchase on the other side of the ledge with the free end," he told Dr. Dodd. The doctor did so. Garry then seized the two lines running out to right and left of him so that they were taut. He then stood on the very edge of the ledge, his back outwards, and allowed the ropes to slide gradually through his hands until at length he was leaning well back over the vertiginous space, his feet still planted firmly on the ledge. He disengaged his hands. The ropes held him. He could use his arms freely.

" It will work," he shouted excitedly. He hauled himself into the ledge again and with feverish haste began making a running noose on a spare rope. Then with the coiled lariat slung over his shoulder he let himself out

3

again until he stood, his body swaying away from the rock face at an alarming angle. He took the lariat and whirled it above his head. It snaked upwards, struck the "cannon," bounced off, and dangled into the gulf. Laboriously he recoiled it and tried again. This time the noose fell over the rock. Gingerly he worked it well down the rock, then gradually applied his weight. His feet came off the ledge and he swung out into space. The rope was secure on the rock and held him fast.

Dr. Dodd's serious face glowed with hope.

"Wonderful, wonderful," was all he could say as he hauled Garry in towards the ledge again.

"Can you climb up that rope?" Garry asked.

"It's not a case of can I," retorted the doctor grimly. "It's a case of got to."

"I'll go first, taking a rope," Garry announced. "You hitch one end to Bourne, then follow me. Between us we can haul him up. We then lower a line to Sir Peter."

"I understand," said the doctor.

Garry slipped off his supporting guy ropes and, fastening another rope about his waist, seized the dangling line firmly. He swung out into space and proceeded to swarm up it. He literally held his life in his hand-grip then. The sun had dropped very low and there was a bitter chill in the air. Garry felt numbness biting into his fingers. His wrists began to tighten up. He was afraid the muscles would bind into cramp. But at last he reached the rock and dragged himself astride it. In another few moments he was on the security of a broad ledge. He could see that the remainder of the ascent was by way of a pile of safe, well-broken-up rocks.

"O.K.," he shouted, and watched the doctor swing out from the cliff face. Slowly the older man climbed, until Garry could grab a shoulder and assist him to safety. The doctor shuddered.

"Heavens, what a nightmare! I don't think I could shin up a rope like that again for a million pounds."

" I was too darn cold to worry about being scared,"
Garry said. " Have you fastened the other end of the
rope to Bourne ? "

" I have."

" Well, let's have him up."

Bourne was very heavy. Hauling him up that twenty
feet was a tremendous strain, but at last they accomplished it ; and with Bourne at last safely on the ledge,
they sank down, panting and exhausted. After a space
to recover, they lowered the rope again for Sir Peter.
The leader was much lighter in weight and he was soon
on the ledge too.

" Wonderful show, McGowan," he said. " You've
saved Bourne's life and probably ours too. It was fortunate
indeed I invited you to this party. Your mountaineering may not have been orthodox, but it saved a nasty
situation."

Sir Peter and Garry gripped hands to form a cradle
for Bourne's shoulders while the doctor supported his
legs. That way they clambered laboriously up the
remaining rocks. Bourne was semi-conscious, but with
every unavoidable jolt he gave a gasp of pain. Once
the top was achieved it was comparatively easy going,
but there still remained a three-mile trudge to the road
down steep turf slopes. It was no mean task with a
thirteen-stone man. Halts were frequent, and progress
painfully slow. Dusk came and made the going worse.
There seemed no end to the three miles. Muscles burned
in the agony of the strain. Garry felt that his body was
beginning to refuse to obey his mind.

At last they saw the light of a cottage. It was not far
away, but it seemed an age before they were knocking
at the rough wooden door. The door opened. A short
man stood there, his rugged face thrown into relief by
heavenly, flickering fire-light.

" Well ? " he demanded suspiciously.

" We've had an accident on the mountains," gasped
Sir Peter.

" Come in, come in," said the man, his manner

changing at once. " Blodwyn, Blodwyn," he called, " there has been an accident on the mountains."

A little elderly woman with a lined face hurried in from another room, wiping her hands on her apron. She watched them carry Bourne into the tiny room.

" Indeed he is badly hurt," she murmured. " You must bring him in here. Indeed he must go to bed at once."

She hastily lit a candle at the fire, and ushered them into a bedroom so small there was scarcely even standing-room for them all. With utter relief they lowered Bourne on to the bed. He stirred uneasily.

Sir Peter and Garry went back to the little fire-warmed kitchen and sank on to the floor in utter exhaustion. Garry had never felt so whacked in all his life. It was not till the following morning that he learned how Dr. Dodd, weary as he was, had worked for hours for the comfort of his friend, warming bricks at the fire, wrapping them in towels, and stacking them about the badly shocked body. For Garry and Sir Peter had unwittingly dropped off to sleep on the rush-matted floor, so utterly weary were they. The following morning when they awoke, excruciatingly stiff, they found that the kindly old shepherd and his wife had covered them with blankets.

Dr. Dodd was still asleep on a couch and looking completely worn out. The old lady entered from the kitchen carrying a tray with plates of delicious-smelling bacon and eggs. When the doctor awoke, the first thing he did was to go in to see Bourne.

" He's sleeping," he announced. " And he'll be all right."

He joined the others in wolfing the bacon and eggs. It was one of those occasions when the simplest food far transcends the most luxurious of banquets.

Later in the day an ambulance arrived, the old man having walked to Capel Curig to telephone. Bourne was looking much brighter as they carried him out. He smiled wryly : " I'm afraid this cuts me out of the

Kinchinga party. You'd better take that darn-fool nephew of mine instead."

Garry guessed that must be the young man he had met on the Engadine Express. Well, it was an ill wind, etc.

" Yes," agreed Sir Peter thoughtfully. " He's an excellent man on rock, but a little impetuous. I'll think about it."

Bourne clasped Garry's hand.

" Thanks a lot, McGowan. I owe you a very great deal. If it hadn't been for you I'd not only have been out of the expedition, I'd have been out of everything."

The stretcher slid into the ambulance and the doors were closed. The shepherd and his wife were reluctant to accept any reward for their kindness. They did not need payment for helping a poor fellow-creature who had been hurt. But Sir Peter insisted, and pressed a note into the old man's hand that made the eyes of both of them goggle with astonishment. The three climbers returned to their hotel by car. As they sat in the lounge at lunch an earnest young man approached them.

" Excuse me, sir, I represent the local paper. Could you tell me about the accident, please ? "

Sir Peter looked at Garry and laughed.

" Ask this fellow," he suggested to the young man. " He's Garry McGowan."

" Garry McGowan, indeed to goodness ! " gasped the young man. He turned red, coughed, and retired in hasty embarrassment.

" You've scared him thoroughly just by being Garry McGowan," laughed Sir Peter. " Seriously though, McGowan, I'm deeply indebted to you. We were in a very tough spot. Dodd and I were in danger as well as Bourne."

" Not to mention the fact that I have a certain liking for my own precious skin," added Garry.

" We most certainly could not have left Bourne there alone," went on Sir Peter. " And if we had had to spend a bitter winter night on an exposed mountain ledge we might very well have succumbed. These bodies of ours will stand so much and no more. I suppose now I should offer you the exclusive story of the expedition."

Garry was thoughtful for a few moments. "You're tempting me," he said at last. "But, as I said a moment ago, I had to save my own skin too."

"Don't belittle a wonderful effort, McGowan."

"Do you still feel the same about this publicity business?" Garry asked.

"I do."

"Well, I may be a hard-boiled newspaper man, but it doesn't fit in with my idea of playing the game to exploit an unfortunate accident. I hope you'll change your mind of your own accord."

"You're a good fellow, McGowan," said Sir Peter. "I'm glad to have met you."

Further climbing was now out of the question. Garry caught the afternoon train back to London. He went straight to his rooms, stowed some clothes into two light travelling-bags, got undressed, stewed for a while in a steaming hot bath, set his alarm clock, and then permitted himself the unbelievable luxury of getting his weary body into a soft bed between crisp, clean sheets.

He slept for an unbroken twelve hours. He was still a bit stiff, however, when he rose. But he returned to his rigorous routine of cold shower and brisk rub-down. It made him feel much better. He dressed, grabbed his bags, and took a taxi to the office. He saw Jimmy as he flew up the stairs.

"Good morning, Mr. McGowan," shouted Jimmy. "Do you want any more windows broken?"

"Not to-day, thank you. I'm just off to America. Cheerio!"

"S'long, guv'nor!"

Garry burst into Carmody's office.

"Well, Garry, did you have a nice quiet week-end as I told you to?"

"I did not. I've been trying to break my neck on a

Welsh mountain and freeze to death into the bargain. I didn't succeed."

" Crazy ! " grunted Carmody. " Stark, staring crazy ! "

" I just called in to say au revoir. Anything you want across the pond ? "

" No, nothing I can think of right now. Good luck, Garry. Here, have a cigar."

" Have one yourself," laughed Garry, ramming it into Carmody's mouth when he opened it to say : " Gosh, I keep forgetting."

A few hours later Garry was dozing to the soothing drone of engines in a comfortable seat 6000 feet above the Atlantic.

CHAPTER III

AMERICAN INTERLUDE

THE middle-weight championship aroused no enthusiasm in Garry. He disliked the commercialism of big boxing. Certainly a sportsman of talent should be able to make his sport his living. But in boxing there were too many promoters, too many parasites, all out to fill their pockets by exploiting the real sportsmen who did all the work and took all the punishment. In addition to that, boxing somehow attracted a particularly unhealthy, weedy sort of crowd. Garry often pondered the fact, and could find no explanation. A big boxing-match crowd was akin to a dog-racing crowd. They were loud and vulgar and considered themselves " sports " when they did not even begin to understand the meaning of the word. Garry often asserted : " You get more real sportsmanship in any boys' club with a couple of kids lamming the lights out of each other because they like it than you find in all the title matches in the world."

But an assignment was an assignment. So Garry went along to cover the big fight. Looking around him from the ringside Press seats, he espied an old friend of his—Willard Conn, president of the All-America Sporting Club. Conn was grey and getting somewhat thin on top, but he retained his slim, youthful figure; and a trim grey moustache added confirmation to his air of distinction. Willard Conn probably knew more top-flight sportsmen than anyone else in the world—even including Garry himself. Garry waved to him. He decided to look Conn up after the fight. He was still afire with the possibility of a Kinchinga race, and Conn might be able to put him on to some information about the American expedition.

Contrary to his expectations, Garry enjoyed the fight as a fight. The contestants were well matched, and it was not until the seventeenth round that a decision was reached. Garry felt that each of the scrappers was more concerned with winning the fight than with winning a handsome purse, which was as it should be. In any case they earned their money.

Garry wrote his story in shorthand as the fight progressed. His style was famous. A McGowan report was terse, very much to the point, and punctuated with characteristically incisive humorous touches. By the time the referee's voice had bawled the count of ten Garry's story was finished. He gathered up his sheaf of copy and pushed through the roaring crowd towards Willard Conn.

Conn extended his hand. " Glad to see you, McGowan," he shouted above the uproar. " I haven't seen you this side of the water for ages. What have you been doing with yourself, you old son-of-a-gun ? "

" It's not what I've been doing with myself," Garry shouted back. " It's what that old headline-splasher Carmody has been doing with me—shooting me off all over the place."

" Been covering this fight ? " Conn asked at the top of his voice.

" Yes," screamed Garry. " Say, I want to have a talk with you, Mr. Conn. I wonder if we could find some place a bit quieter than this ? "

" Sure we can. Come and have supper with me at the Club."

" Sounds a swell idea to me," shouted Garry. " But I've got to get my story across first. They'll be holding up the presses for it. It's getting on into the wee small hours on the other side of the Atlantic, remember. We're six hours ahead of you. And that paper's got to get out in time for Mr. Everyman all over England to read it over breakfast."

" I understand," grinned Conn. " Will you be long ? "

" Maybe half an hour. I'm phoning it."

" Well, it will be some time before I get away myself. Ask one of the commissionaires to show you my Cadillac. They all know it."

" Good," shouted Garry, and waved au revoir.

He fought his way through the milling crowd to the Press room, and found a vacant telephone booth.

" Operator, give me long distance," he said. " Yes, long distance—London. I want the call charged to the New York office of the London *Morning Gazette*. . . . Hullo, is that London ? . . . Give me Temple Bar four-one-three-two, please. . . . *Gazette ?* Extension two-two, please. . . . That you, Greg ? McGowan here."

" You're late," he heard Carmody's voice crackle at the other end. " I switched off the radio at the end of the fight five minutes ago."

" You sure want your news hot. Next fight I cover I'll write the story first and then they can fight it out according to the way I write it."

" Cut the tomfoolery," rasped Carmody's voice. " I've got a hundred thousand pounds' worth of machinery held up for that story."

" O.K.," said Garry. " I start shooting. It will run about a full column. You'd better double it up with a double-column heading. Fifteen inches d.c. space should cover it."

He faintly heard Carmody's voice calling the composing-room on another phone and giving the necessary instructions.

" O.K.," came Carmody's voice on the outside receiver. " Shoot. And don't forget my shorthand's getting rusty. I can only make a hundred and twenty words a minute."

Garry dictated his story and hung up.

He had no trouble in locating Conn's Cadillac. Conn was in it and waiting.

" Well, what's the trouble? " he asked, as the chauffeur let out the clutch.

" It's not really trouble," Garry said. " It's just that I'm very interested in this expedition to Kinchinga that the Mercer Press is organizing."

" Mountain-climbing is a little off your usual beat, isn't it ? " asked Conn.

" Maybe it is, a little," Garry agreed.

" You're usually nosing about for a contest, man against man, machine against machine. Mountaineering scarcely comes within the accepted meaning of the word ' sport.' "

" That's true to a certain extent," conceded Garry. " But there is the basic element of sport in it. Only instead of man against man, it's man against the forces of Nature."

" Agreed. But, without labouring the point too much, I would like to suggest that a race to the summit of Kinchinga, for instance, would come more within the meaning of the term. You're not trying to organize a rival expedition, are you ? I wouldn't put it past you, you young rascal. Think of it—an Anglo-American race to the summit of Kinchinga. It's the sort of story you'd give your right hand to cover."

Garry glanced at him sharply. However, the alternating light and gloom as the street lamps flashed by revealed only an amused half-smile, and Garry was pretty sure he had heard no whisper of the Rawson expedition.

" What do you know about the Mercer stunt ? " Garry demanded.

" Very little, I'm afraid," said Conn. " But I may be able to put you in touch with someone who does."

The car swished to a halt. Garry and Conn alighted and entered the spacious, luxurious hall of the All-America Sporting Club's headquarters. They went to supper in the restaurant, and over the meal discussed the evening's fight.

Garry was talking when Conn cut him short.

" I say," he said. " Here's the very man you want."

Garry turned to follow the direction of his gaze and saw a moderately-sized man with incredibly broad, powerful shoulders, which were accentuated by a well-cut tuxedo. He had apparently just entered, and was waiting for an attendant to lead him to a table.

" Excuse me," said Conn, and, rising, strode across the room to the newcomer, shook his hand, and escorted him back to where Garry sat.

" McGowan," said Conn, " I want you to meet Carr Davies, president of the National Mountaineering Society."

Garry rose and shook hands.

" Glad to know you, McGowan," boomed Davies in a deep, slow voice. " I've heard quite a bit about you. Conn tells me you want the dope on this Mercer expedition to Kinchinga."

" Yes, I'm very interested," said Garry.

" Well," drawled Davies, an expression of uncertainty on his face as he seated himself, " I might say at the outset that we mountaineers of the old school strongly disapprove of the whole affair."

" I understand the men making the trip are all very young," said Garry.

" Too young," said Davies.

" It's not just middle-age being a little jealous of youth ? " suggested Garry slyly. Davies must have been between forty and fifty.

" Nothing of the kind," returned Davies, a trifle indignantly. " I'll tell you how the whole affair started. It was out in the Big Horn Mountains. Three youths from one of the towns in the district were pretty fond of climbing. They were just ordinary young fellows working at ordinary jobs. They couldn't afford expensive equipment or expensive fees for climbing clubs. And they certainly couldn't afford to travel to the famous mountain-climbing districts of the world. Still, they got a lot of fun clambering up and down their local peaks. They did it because they loved mountains. Now, that's the right spirit. Given experience and guidance by older and well-skilled mountaineers, no doubt they would develop into fine climbers.

" Well, these kids got ambitious. About fifty miles from their home town is Mount Macarthur. It's one of the finest peaks in that part of the world—it tops ten thousand feet—and some of our best-known climbers have put in some very good work on it. But no one has ever climbed the south face. For one thing, a mountaineer is not a suicide, and any half-boiled climber can tell that the rock there is as brittle as Venetian glass and as treacherous as a rattlesnake.

" These kids, then, reckoned they would climb that south face. The fools were rushing in where angels feared to tread. They had all the confidence of youth, and no fear at all. They packed some camping-gear into the old Ford belonging to the father of one of them, and set out for Mount Macarthur. They went as far as they could in the old tin buggy, first by road, and then by rough tracks, and they were then within striking distance of the mountain. They camped the night, and next day they set out to climb the south face.

" And, by luck, they did it. I don't know how they did it. No one does. They're not quite sure how they did it themselves. They got pretty scared, but it was more dangerous to go back than to go on. So they went on. They did what every climbing expert in the country said was impossible. They climbed the south face of Mount Macarthur."

" Jolly fine show," commented Garry. " They must be born climbers. Just the type for an expedition like Kinchinga—youth, courage, determination."

" Rot," snorted Davies. " That climb was pure luck.

I'll grant they could never have done it without youth, courage, and determination. But they want a darn sight more than that for a Himalayan expedition. In the Himalayas it's experience that counts. The danger there is not in a hazardous climb of a few hours' duration, but in the protracted exposure to the forces of storm and cold and thin air and dizzy heights for weeks or months on end. It is experience and well-trained, disciplined minds that count there. One impetuous false move might very easily mean death to the whole party. And as for sending three inexperienced youths on such a project, well, it's criminally idiotic."

"How did the proposal for the expedition come about?" Garry asked.

"It happened a journalist of the Mercer combine was on vacation in the district. Naturally the climb caused a lot of excitement and comment locally, and this journalist couldn't help but hear of it. Well, he got an idea. He didn't know the first thing about mountaineering, but he had read something about Kinchinga. Then, he thought, here was material for a terrific circulation-boosting story. Everyone dreams of taking part in Himalayan expeditions and Arctic explorations and record-breaking flights and so on. But it's only the fortunate few who can. So this journalist worked it out that if he took three ordinary young fellows like these, three ordinary young fellows just like millions of other young fellows in America, and gave them such an opportunity, everyone would think : ' There but for the grace of God go I.' It would arouse terrific interest. Everyone would want to know everything about the expedition.

"The story would be exclusive to the Mercer Press. Just think what that would mean. The story of the expedition from beginning to end would cover several months. The circulation of the Mercer newspapers would grow tremendously as people bought them to follow the story. It would certainly be dramatic—three ordinary young men attacking one of the world's

mightiest mountains. And for good measure they
plug that arrant nonsense about the Monster of
Kinchinga.

" Naturally the lads fell for the idea and fell heavily.
What lads wouldn't ? But I tell you, McGowan, this
expedition is phoney. The Mercer combine isn't out to
encourage mountaineering and youthful aspiration. It's
only out to fill its bank account—nothing else.

" If those young fellows succeed in getting to any
height at all on the mountain they'll be as good as dead.
They're raw and inexperienced, and it's little short of
murder to send them there. My colleagues and I have
done our best to scotch the expedition, but the Mercer
group is terrifically strong and we are powerless. The
whole thing is a rotten publicity stunt. It's worse than
that. For the sake of a few thousand dollars those people
are sending three fine youths to almost certain death.
In fact, I guess they wouldn't mind much if the lads did
die. It would make a super scoop as a climax to the
whole business—a syrupy, vulgar story of American
youth perishing gloriously in high adventure. The
whole thing makes me sick."

Davies expressed his opinions with a vehement sincerity. Garry became very thoughtful.

" It does sound like a pretty filthy stunt," he agreed.
He decided there and then to see these youths before he
returned to London.

The following day he phoned Carmody.

" Greg, expect me when you see me."

What sounded like an explosion occurred in the
diaphragm of the receiver. Garry grinned. At last the
voice in London grew coherent.

" I've got a job for you," spluttered Carmody. " And
you've got to come and cover it."

" I'm chasing a little job on my own account."

"You come back here," warned Carmody. "Or . . ."

" When I'm ready, Greg," said Garry. " And take it
easy. Remember what the doctor said about your blood
pressure."

" If you're not back by to-morrow night," raved Carmody, " you're fired."

" Good," returned Garry. He had been fired a score of times. " The *News-Courier* have been pestering me to go to them for months. I'll give them a ring right away."

Carmody's voice was at once placating—and with reason. He knew full well that Garry had a tremendous following. His salary and his expenses as he chased about the world cost the *Gazette* a great deal of money ; but the number of people who bought the *Gazette* just for the McGowan column made it well worth while.

" Now, Garry, you don't want to take it that way," soothed Carmody. " Garry, if you'll . . ."

Garry grinned mischievously. He would give Greg something to worry about. It did him good to have a dampener now and again. So he hung up. Two hours later he was in a transcontinental Douglas air-liner bound for Grantville.

It was not hard to find the three heroes of the Mount Macarthur climb. Everyone seemed to know them. Everyone was proud of them, proud that three stalwart sons of Grantville were to attack the unconquerable Kinchinga. An official at the airport told him : " You go along Main Street till you come to Elmer's Service Station—that's young Larry Elmer's old man's joint. Larry works in the repair shop. Darn clever kid he is with motors, too."

The official hailed a decrepit Ford van that was just pulling out laden with baggage, bound piles of newspapers, two indignant live geese in a wooden crate, and other miscellaneous items. " Hey, Luke ! " he shouted, " you might drop this guy off'n Main Street. He come all the way from England to see young Larry. That youngster sure is getting famous."

" Yeah," shouted back the white-bearded driver with an old cracked voice. He looked as decrepit as, and considerably more ancient than, his vehicle—and that was saying something. " I just been over to Hawkstone.

That's sixty mile away. They even heard about 'im over there. I never guessed them kids' durn silly climbin' hills'd cause such a galumphing.''

" Galumphing ? " asked Garry.

" Yeah, galumphing. I invented the word meself, I did. It's a durn good word. I offered it to *Webster's Dictionary*, but they turned it down. Them fellers don't know a good word when they see it.''

" It's a very good word,'' agreed Garry, putting on a serious countenance to hide the grin that threatened to crease up his face. He climbed on to the seat beside the driver. One of the springs had done its best to escape from the restriction of the leather covering, and every jolt—and there were many of them—forcibly reminded Garry of the fact.

" You one o' them writer guys ? " asked the old man.

" Guilty,'' Garry owned up.

" And ye want to see young Larry Elmer ? "

" That was roughly the idea.''

" Then ye're wastin' yer time. That feller Kell from Mercer's *Leader* won't let them tell nothin' to no other writer fellers. He says it's excloosive, if ye know what that means.''

" I can guess,'' replied Garry. " And who is Kell ? "

" Him ? He's that reporter guy that thought up the idea o' sendin' them youngsters to climb that pimple with a durn silly name.''

" Well, it's a bit bigger than a pimple,'' Garry told him.

" You can't tell me,'' said the old-timer. " I guess these hills we got here'd take a power o' beatin'. I went to Noo York once when I was a young feller, an' I never seed nothin' to beat 'em. Ye cover a mighty lot o' ground between here an' Noo York. I guess them mountains of ours is jist about the biggest in the world.''

Garry did not try to disillusion him. The old man wouldn't believe the Himalayas were more than two and a half times as high as his hills anyway.

" Well, here y'are, mister,'' the old man said as his car,

with a groan and a rattle and a squawk of brakes, lurched to a halt. " That there's young Larry's father's joint."

" Good," said Garry, and thankfully lifted himself from the rebellious spring and alighted. " Thanks a lot—and here, buy yourself some Coca-Colas at the drug-store down the street."

" Thank ye, mister. And by the way, you bein' by way o' bein' a writer, ye might care to remember that word galumphing. It's a durn good word." He waved, and his ancient motor jerked violently into motion and rattled down the street, scaring the life out of all the dogs of the town, who bolted for shelter behind paling fences and barked furiously at it as it passed.

Garry walked into the service station. It seemed deserted, except for a pair of legs protruding from under a car.

" I say," said Garry.

" You wanting gas ? " asked a voice from under the car.

" No ; I'm looking for a chap called Larry Elmer."

" That's me," said the voice.

" Well, come out and let's have a look at you."

The legs wriggled, and a body slithered out. A face capped by a fair, tousled mop, soiled here and there by smudges of black grease, looked up at him.

" Are you a reporter ? " asked Larry Elmer.

" I am," Garry admitted.

" Then I can't tell you anything. Mr. Kell said we're tied by contract to his combine."

" Yes, I know all that."

" Then why did you come here ? "

" I was interested—not merely as a reporter. I heard about your Mount Macarthur climb."

" You're not an American, are you ? "

" No. I'm McGowan, of the London *Morning Gazette*."

" And you heard about it all the way over there ? "

" I did."

The lad's face broke into a grin—a pleased, open sort

4

of grin that Garry liked. Larry Elmer was only about nineteen. He had a well-built body. His face was brown from much sun and open air, and a few freckles made him look still more boyish. He had keen eyes, and a strong, determined chin.

" Gosh," exclaimed Larry. " Can you imagine that ! Can you imagine it ! " He made to shake Garry's hand and suddenly remembered his own greasy paws. His mouth curled into a sheepish smile. " Aw shucks, I got so sort of carried away I forgot my dirty hands."

" Who are your pals ? " asked Garry.

" There's Ted Cray and Tex Butcher."

" Are they the same age as you ? "

" No ; they're a bit older. They're both twenty. Ted works out on his pa's farm and Tex works in the bank up the road."

" And you're the leader of the expedition ? "

" Sure. Gee, it's just too good to believe ! We just go out on a climb like we do most week-ends, and suddenly we're famous and going on an expedition to the Himalayas."

" Don't you think you're taking a risk ? You're young and inexperienced."

" Inexperienced ? We've been climbing mountains round here for six years. And we're plenty tough. Just you feel that." He doubled up his arm and hardened his biceps.

" Say, that's pretty good," said Garry appreciatively.

" Sure," nodded Larry.

" But you want more than that," Garry told him. " You've never been on a big expedition. You've never had any experience of the tremendous organization that is necessary."

" Mr. Kell is looking after the organization," explained Larry. " All we've got to do is climb."

" When are you going ? "

" We're leaving here in about two weeks."

" I see," mused Garry. " So, in less than a month this Mr. Kell is organizing the whole thing ? "

" He's a live wire is Mr. Kell," Larry said. " He doesn't let any grass grow under his feet."

" No," agreed Garry, his mouth setting into a thin grim line. " Listen, Larry, I know just how you feel about all this. I'd be crazy myself to have a slam at such a trip. But look at it this way. Every Himalayan expedition has required long months of preparation. The whole affair is miles removed from the sort of climbing you've been used to. So how can your Mr. Kell prepare for it in a few weeks ? I'm the last person in the world to discourage youth from seizing its chance of high adventure. I don't want you to think I'm just a busybody poking my nose in where it doesn't belong, because I'm not. You're a fine type of fellow, Larry. America needs lads like you. And I'd hate to see you die just so some newspaper combine that is out for itself alone can make a grand pile of dollars."

" I don't get it," said Larry.

" This expedition is suicide."

Larry smiled. " We're tough. We reckon we can get up that hill all right. We're not scared."

" Yes, I know it's going to be fun. But I tell you it's more than dangerous. If you get high up on that mountain you'll die. I mean that."

" We can look after ourselves," Larry assured him.

Garry was exasperated. To attack the supreme confidence of youth is always exasperating. It's like trying to ladle out the ocean.

" Larry," said Garry desperately, " Kell and his combine are making suckers of you. They're not sending you to Kinchinga because they like you. They're sending you because it's the devil of a good story. They don't care whether you're killed or not. They're going to sell an awful lot of papers to people who are breaking their necks to know all about you. That's all they want. They're not troubling even to make adequate preparation."

" Is that so ? " asked a smooth, silky voice behind Garry. He swung round to see a youngish man smiling at him. It was the smile that struck Garry first. He did not like it. It was twisted, sarcastic. Then Garry took in the other details of the man—the exaggerated padding of the shoulders of his suit flattering an unhealthy flat-chested figure ; the perfumed, over-oiled black hair with a wave that could only have been created by a machine ; the tiny curved moustache that was ridiculously affected. Garry disliked them all.

" This is Mr. Kell," introduced Larry.

" How do you do, stranger," said Kell. " I—er—did not catch the name."

" My name's McGowan."

" Not the great Garry McGowan ? "

" I am Garry McGowan."

" Ah, the great apostle of clean sport, the weeder-out of sporting scandals, the great, big, clean, healthy man himself ! "

Garry didn't like the smooth, sarcastic tone.

" And you are the organizing genius behind this suicide stunt," said Garry.

Kell's smile froze. " I don't like that, McGowan."

" I didn't think you would," barked Garry. " You know as well as I do that this stunt is just a circulation-booster. It's phoney. You're just sending these lads to their deaths so that you can sell more copies of your rotten papers."

" Wild words, McGowan. Dangerous words. There's a law of libel, you know. And what do you propose doing about it ? And what's it got to do with you anyway ? You suggest my organization is phoney. Well, the organization is my responsibility. And if I have been able to complete preparations in so short a time it only shows what a lot of old women have been behind other Himalayan expeditions with their ridiculous everlasting fussing."

" Look here," burst out Garry angrily, " you have never climbed a mountain in your life. What do you know about these things ? I suppose you'd call a fine mountaineer like Sir Peter Rawson an old woman, you impudent pipsqueak. And he took nearly two years preparing his Kinchinga expedition."

Kell was immediately alert.

" So Sir Peter Rawson is having a crack at Kinchinga too," he crooned.

Garry felt his blood rising. In his anger he had unwittingly let the cat out of the bag.

" That is not for publication," he said.

" No, of course not," agreed the oily voice. " I see now why the white knight crusading for a clean Press was so anxious to dissuade these intrepid young Americans from making this ascent. Youth and energy and live-wire organization have certain obvious advantages over a crowd of middle-aged old women. It would be so galling to British prestige to be beaten to one of the few big mountain prizes left in the world."

" You're barking up the wrong tree," snapped Garry. " And that sort of talk doesn't help Anglo-American relationships. A certain representative of Great Britain might be strongly tempted to punch a certain representative of the United States on the nose—and hard."

Kell smiled a trifle palely, and backed away a little.

Garry turned to young Elmer. "You think about what I told you, Larry," he said. " I like you, son, and I'd hate you to be a sucker on that snake's account."

" We're not going to miss an opportunity like this," Larry said. " You bet your life we're not. No one in the world could talk us out of it. Would you give up a chance like this yourself ? "

Garry considered a moment. " No," he replied wryly, and turned and walked out.

The following morning Garry read the following in one of the Mercer newspapers :

> " A certain well-known English sports writer has been trying to dissuade Lawrence Elmer and his friends from their projected attack on Kinchinga. His objections to the attempt were those which have already been put forward from several sources— that this is a mere sensation stunt, that it is ethically wrong to send these young men on such a hazardous venture. His efforts were unavailing.

" It transpires that Sir Peter Rawson, the noted English climber, has also been preparing an expedition to Kinchinga. One wonders whether that aforementioned writer's intentions were so high-minded as he asserted they were. Britons are jealous of their reputations as mountaineers, and to be beaten to the summit of Kinchinga by a party of American youngsters would be a severe blow to British pride.

" We once again take the opportunity of stressing that our policy is to assist young America, to seek out talent and ability, and to give that talent and ability opportunity where opportunity would normally never arise. And once again we stress that youth in high adventure is a great and glorious thing, symbolizing the spirit of our nation. There is too little of the spirit of quest in the world to-day, too little of that grand old pioneering spirit that has sent men into the great, silent, unknown corners of the earth . . ."

The mealy hypocrisy made Garry sick. In a rage he crushed the paper and flung it across the room. He wished, as he clenched his big fist, that Kell were in the room with him at that very moment.

When he quietened down again, however, he realized that the last paragraph, at any rate, was perfectly true with regard to youth and high adventure. But there was no sincerity in the man who wrote it.

CHAPTER IV

SIR PETER GIVES WAY

Some days later Garry arrived back in London. He went straight to Carmody.

" Hullo, Greg," he said as he opened the door.

Carmody looked up and grunted.

" Sit down," he said, quietly and slowly.

Garry sat, and noticed how he puffed his cigarette quickly. There was trouble in the air—and plenty of it.

" McGowan," Carmody said, " you're fired."

" O.K.," shrugged Garry and rose.

" Sit down," barked Carmody hastily. " I've got things to tell you."

" If I'm no longer on the staff of the *Gazette* I don't think they'll interest me." Garry was quite sure Carmody would not let him go. He was quite sure of his own worth in Fleet Street. On occasions he was not beyond playing up his value to the *Gazette* in order to win a point. Maybe such behaviour had some of the earmarks of blackmail, but when Carmody got into his pig-headed moods Garry considered such methods justifiable. Nevertheless, he knew in his heart that he could not abandon the *Gazette* if it came to the pinch. The *Gazette* had given him his first big chance, and he had a great affection for it.

Garry reached the door.

" Garry," ordered Carmody. " Don't be an ass. You just sit down there."

" Then I'm not sacked ? "

" You win," Carmody conceded grudgingly. " But I warn you. There's a limit to what I can stand."

" You've told me that—well, I should think this is about the fifteenth time you have told me."

" And one of these days I'll reach the limit and you'll really find yourself looking for another job. And now——"

" All right, skip the lecture, Greg. I know what's coming. I could probably tell you word for word what you're going to say. And maybe you'd be right."

" Sir Peter Rawson rang up a few days ago. I thought he would fuse every telephone line in London. He was in the very deuce of a temper. Now, I don't know what you've been up to, but I gather you did meet Sir Peter after all ? "

" I did."

Carmody scratched his head.

" Heaven only knows how you did it," he breathed, almost in admiration. " But the point seems to be he told you in strict confidence that he was actually preparing an expedition to Kinchinga."

" Yes, he did."

" And you've blown the gaff in the States and caused a first-class stir. I can't understand it. I don't get it at all. I don't have to remind you that the greatest sin a newspaper man can commit is to betray a confidence."

" I know all that, Greg. And you needn't think I'm feeling particularly chirpy right now. I've got to see Sir Peter and apologize. And you needn't think I'm looking forward to it with the eagerness of a kid on Christmas Eve."

" But why did you do it ? Why ? "

" Because I couldn't help myself. Have you ever been in a flaming-red raw rage ? "

" Don't ask silly questions. You know perfectly well I never lose my head."

Garry let that pass. " Well, I was in a temper, and it slipped out without my realizing it."

" A newspaper man should know better than to lose his temper."

" Then must a newspaper man be entirely inhuman ? "

" Yes."

" Rot ! If any decent man can swallow this sort of racket without seeing red, then I'll swim to the South Seas and rot away the rest of my life on a desert island," snapped Garry. He told Carmody the inside story of the Mercer expedition as organized by Kell.

" The dirty hound ! " roared Carmody when he had finished. He got to his feet and paced the room. " That's the sort of thing that's killing clean journalism. It doesn't matter what you do or what you print so long as your paper sells—that's their principle. It's the sort of cheap sensationalism we honest journalists have to put up with. I'm going to chuck the news game. I'm going to go into Parliament. I'll wipe the yellow press off the face of the earth." He grew purple in the face.

" Sit down, Greg," Garry suggested. " It doesn't become a newspaper man to lose his temper."

" I'm perfectly calm and collected," roared Carmody, plumping into a chair.

" You're forgetting the Mercer Press is in America, and you can't do anything about it."

" It's not only the Mercer Press. The cheap screamer headline press in London is just as bad. They're getting all the dope from the Mercer crowd, and screaming their heads off in flash headlines. In the meantime Sir Peter continues his policy of behaving like a well-bred oyster. And we who try to keep journalism honest and decent have got to sit by quietly because we refuse to publish rumours or anything but properly authenticated facts."

" We can beat their vulgar shouting only by publishing the true facts of the case," Garry said.

" What do you mean—true facts ? "

" By telling the public that the Mercer expedition is a cheap circulation-boosting stunt based on risking the lives of three decent lads."

" Meanwhile the cheap press has got in first, and is telling the English public what the Mercer Press is telling the American. They're telling them that any objections we may make are inspired by jealousy, that Sir Peter and his kind delight to invest mountaineering with a lot of mumbo-jumbo, and are afraid their prestige will suffer if a few American youngsters with no pretensions to expert knowledge can conquer Kinchinga. The sensation-mongers are screaming for a race between the two expeditions."

" They would ! "

" So you don't approve of a race ? "

" Of course I don't."

" I thought you were all for it. You were shouting about what a story it would make."

" I didn't know the true facts then. Two properly organized and serious expeditions in a contest like that is one thing. But a race between a party of experienced men and a bunch of green youths who have never been on

a real mountain in their lives is another thing altogether.
It's criminal."

" It's within the law."

" There are plenty of things within the law that are
criminal just the same. I'm going to see Sir Peter."

" I'd put on a couple of bullet-proof vests if I were you.
I gather he'd like your hide for a doormat."

Garry took a taxi to Sir Peter's house in Kensington.
He felt very hot under the collar. Never had he so
dreaded an interview. His ring on the doorbell was
answered by Sir Peter's suave little secretary.

" Oh yes," said the secretary, with a hint of a super-
cilious smile. " Mr. McGowan, of course. Yes, I'm
sure Sir Peter will see you. I understand he is rather
anxious to renew acquaintance with you. Wait here,
will you, please ? "

The man's manner only made Garry feel worse. He
seemed as though he were taking a malevolent delight
in the discomfiture the interview would bring to Garry.
After a seeming age, Sir Peter appeared. His face showed
no emotion whatever.

" I had to see you, sir," said Garry, rising to his feet.

" No doubt," agreed Sir Peter dryly. " I suppose you
have a full and complete explanation ? "

" You must take a pretty poor view of me," Garry
ventured. " I let the cat out of the bag all right."

" Not to mention a lot of nasty publicity—which is, of
course, nice meaty food for you news-hounds."

" It wasn't intentional. I lost my temper with a nasty
piece of work while I was over in the States and it slipped
out. I've come to apologize   I never dreamt even then
that there would be such a fuss."

" I don't intend to waste any time," said Sir Peter.
" Naturally I was extremely angry that you should let
me down. I hate to be found wrong in my estimation of
character. So I hope your explanation is a good one."

" I can explain all right," said Garry eagerly. " And
there's something else too. I want you to drop all this
secrecy."

" There doesn't seem to be much secrecy," Sir Peter commented meaningly. " I think I explained that my desire to climb Kinchinga was purely personal. Yet my intentions are now being bandied about the front pages of the slush press. I am being accused of attempting to institute a campaign to dissuade the Americans from making their attempt. I am accused of being afraid of being beaten. As I told you once before, I have no desire for publicity. I do not care if I am beaten to Kinchinga summit by a funicular railway carrying thousands of tourists. I want to climb it for purely personal gratification. You can imagine I'm not particularly overjoyed at the present vulgar fuss."

" Yes, I know, Sir Peter," Garry agreed. " I regret it sincerely. And yet I've got to ask you to let me tell your story to the world in a straightforward way."

" What ? " barked Sir Peter, almost losing his equanimity.

" It's the only way to clean up the whole messy business. I let the cat out of the bag unwittingly. But it's out now. I'll tell you how it happened. It's a fairly long story. I first got the strength of the Mercer stunt from Carr Davies, the President of the United States National Mountaineering Society."

" Yes, I know him," interposed Sir Peter. " Well, you'd better sit down and tell me the whole tale of woe."

" Well, Carr Davies told me how the business started, and I went to Grantville especially to see those lads."

Garry explained Davies's views on the expedition, about his meeting with young Larry Elmer and with Kell. He told Sir Peter the circumstances under which he had impulsively mentioned his own projected expedition.

" I'm sorry it happened," Garry concluded. " But it's happened, and there's nothing we can do about it. Now do you understand why I want you to make your plans public ? "

" I'm blessed if I do."

" This is the main point. Those lads are victims of a

cruel circulation-boosting stunt. They're naturally not going to chuck away such a chance of adventure. I wouldn't if I were in their place. And you wouldn't either. But that doesn't make things right. There's no way of stopping that stunt except by getting to the top of Kinchinga first. That would mean that the Mercer stunt would lose its point. Your success would completely eclipse it. Then they'd call it off."

" Rather discouraging for the youngsters, eh ? " observed Sir Peter.

" I agree. But remember, they're raw mountaineers. You know better than I do just how much experience counts on these picnics. Those kids would be killed if they got to any height."

" Unless they were incredibly lucky. I don't think they would get high enough to get into danger. I imagine they'd turn back before that. They'd be too scared."

" Maybe they would," agreed Garry. "But they'd go on just the same. I don't often make a mistake. And I'd say those kids are the sort who'd die rather than have anyone accuse them of being scared. They're fine types of lads—the sort of youngsters America can well be proud of."

" And no doubt your desire to give publicity to my expedition is quite, quite impersonal ? "

Garry grinned wryly. " I'm an ink-slinger," he explained. " I've got ink in my veins and telephone wires for nerves. It would be a story you'd ask for on bended knees. I own up to it. I'm darn excited about it. But that's not all. Journalism deals with people. You tell the world about people—people doing pretty marvellous things as well as people doing pretty foul things. There are some things that happen to people and things that they do that are just plain dull. Other things make big news. A journalist can smell a good story a mile off. But sometimes you can hurt people by telling the world about them. It's like putting a spotlight on them. They can't escape from the light. Some people, of course, just revel in being in the limelight. Others are shy, retiring sorts. The light tortures them, if you get what I mean.

" If you've got a heart in you at all you use discretion. If the story's going to harm anyone you just forget it. That's why I didn't take advantage of your offer when you proposed letting me have the story rights of your expedition as a reward for getting your friend Bourne out of a fix. I wanted the story all right. But you shied away from publicity, and I don't like the idea of turning an unfortunate accident to my own advantage. Whether I'm a newshound or not, I would have done everything I could to save Bourne, and I'm not asking you to come into the spotlight on the strength of it.

" I'm asking you to give me the story rights now, because if I can splash it before the eyes of the whole world it will do a lot to push the Mercer stunt into the background. You, at least, have a chance of conquering Kinchinga. And if you do, the whole Mercer build-up loses its point. The Mercer Press is screaming to high heaven what a wonderful organization it is to give such opportunities to youth. Well, maybe it gives opportunities, but only because it means pennies in its own money-box. And it doesn't much care if those kids do perish. It's to give this rotten sort of journalism a poke in the eye that I'm asking you to let me write up your expedition."

Garry had warmed up to his speech, and his voice was resonant with righteous indignation. He suddenly realized that he had even been a little melodramatic. His frown dissolved, and he grinned shyly.

" Sorry to shout the house down," he said. " But dirty play always acts on me like a red rag, and I reckon this is dirty play."

" That's all right, McGowan," said Sir Peter. " I'm glad to learn you didn't just betray a confidence when you let the cat out of the bag."

" Then you do believe me ? "

Sir Peter smiled. " I can just see you getting all worked up about this Kell fellow. I hate the vulgarity of certain sections of the Press just as much as you do. I suppose that is why I am so violently opposed to publicity as regards myself. But you've given me another angle on the subject. I wonder if you've ever tried selling vacuum cleaners ? "

" Why ? "

" You would be a great success at it. You have considerable powers of persuasion. You have persuaded me that in the interests of decent journalism I should let the world know all about my plans and progress."

It was all Garry could do to refrain from whooping with delight.

" I'm not going to suggest that you accompany me to the summit of Kinchinga," continued Sir Peter. " That is a job for a select few. A considerable party and scores of porters work for months so that the select few might stand on the summit for a few minutes. It sounds rather stupid, doesn't it ? "

" If you put it that way, it does," agreed Garry. " But it's the spirit of the thing that really matters—the great satisfaction of setting out to do a hard job and doing it."

" Exactly. I may not even get to the summit myself. It depends on circumstances and the physical state of the party as to who makes the final attempt. Naturally I hope I will be one of them. So you see, I can't promise that you will come to the top with us. But I invite you to join our party. It is not beyond your powers, so far as I can see, to accompany us at least as far as our base camp. Beyond that, I'm afraid, I cannot yet say. Our packs are naturally limited, and only those whose presence is essential to our conquering the peak will strike to the highest camps."

" I understand."

" You will come ? "

" I'm already on the way," cried Garry exultantly. He shook Sir Peter's hand vigorously. " Thanks a lot."

" We sail for India on Thursday fortnight."

Garry rushed back to the *Gazette's* offices and barged into Carmody's den with all the exuberance of a high-speed tank run wild. Carmody, who was just emerging from his office, caught the full force of the swinging door and bounced backwards nursing a funny-bone that was not at all funny just then.

" Greg," shouted Garry, " behold the *Gazette*'s special correspondent with the Rawson Kinchinga expedition. I'm sailing for Calcutta in a fortnight."

" You can sail to Timbuctoo," howled Carmody, " you overgrown offspring of a rogue elephant. You can sail to Hades and I'll buy you a one-way ticket. You can . . ." Realization seeped through Carmody's anger and at last reached his brain. " You're going where ? " he demanded.

" India."

" You mean you've bearded the dragon in his den ? "

" I have."

" You're a walking miracle, McGowan. I don't know how you do it. The devil himself must have been somewhere in your ancestry. . . . But listen, you can't go to India."

" You'll have to find some pretty powerful chains to hold me back. And anyway, why can't I go ? "

" There's the football cup-finals in five weeks' time."

" They can look after themselves."

" And there's the billiards title-match in three weeks."

" Suppose I were to walk out of this office right into an accident and spend six months in hospital ? "

" Don't suggest such things," urged Carmody. " I don't believe in tempting fate."

Garry laughed.

" I guess the *Gazette* would manage to come out every morning without me somehow or other. Give someone else a break."

" Mountain-climbing isn't in your line," protested Carmody. " It isn't a sport."

" Then what is it ? " demanded Garry. " An industry ? "

" In Switzerland it is ! "

" Look here, we're wasting breath. I've appointed myself the *Gazette*'s special correspondent on this outing. And that's that."

" Who's boss round here ? "

" You are, Mr. Carmody, please, sir. But you take what copy I give you and like it."

Garry took delight in tormenting Carmody, knowing well enough that Greg would not dare sack him even if he really wanted to. As a matter of fact, the two had a deep mutual respect and even affection, but neither would admit as much to the other.

" Indeed ? " roared Carmody. " I'll soon alter that. To-morrow you cover the big match at Wembley."

" And, please, sir, can I go to India, sir ? "

" No," thundered Carmody.

" You're not going to let a story like that slide ? "

" Of course not," Carmody snapped. " Devlin is a good descriptive writer. He could do it hands down."

" O.K.," shrugged Garry.

" And I want that copy for the Wembley match early," he shouted after Garry as he went out.

The following evening Garry sauntered into Carmody's office and tossed a folded manuscript on to his desk. Carmody picked it up and opened it. Garry interested himself in the traffic in the street two storeys below, but out of the corner of his eye he watched Carmody's face as he read the copy. It grew slowly to a rich purple hue and the room became heavy with smoke as he puffed faster and faster at his cigarette.

At last he turned to Garry and spoke very quietly.

" McGowan, you're not the man to waste your own time scribbling nonsense even to pull *my* leg. What's the idea of this ? " He slapped Garry's copy with the back of his hand.

" That's my article for to-morrow's *Gazette*."

" I'm not in the mood for fooling."

" I'm not fooling. That's my copy, and you're just going to love it."

" Do you mean to say you didn't go to that match at all ? "

" I didn't."

" Do you mean to say you haven't a report on one of the most important fixtures of the season ? "

" I sent Fetherley to cover it. He's a promising lad, and he deserves a break."

Carmody rose. " Perhaps you'd like to take the sporting editor's chair," he suggested, indicating the vacant seat. " You seem to think you can run this show."

" Thanks," said Garry cheerfully and sat down, putting his feet on the desk. Carmody puffed his cigarette more furiously than ever.

" Get out of that chair," he roared. He had not imagined for one moment that Garry would commit the sacrilege of accepting the offer.

" Oh no," said Garry. " This seat fits me very comfortably."

He rang the bell on the desk.

" Have you taken leave of your senses ? " Carmody roared.

" I've taken just about as much as I can stand."

A knock on the door coincided with its opening, and Jimmy entered.

" You rang, Mr. Carmo—" He caught sight of Garry in Carmody's chair, shot a quick, apprehensive glance at Carmody, whose visage presented all the menace of a seething volcano, and said, " Hullo, Mr. McGowan."

" Hullo, Jimmy," responded Garry. " Take this copy to the composing-room, will you," and he handed Jimmy the copy that had caused Carmody such a rash of temper.

Jimmy took the copy and was gone before Carmody could splutter into coherence.

" You're stark crazy, McGowan. I won't publish it."

" You will," grinned Garry. " And my public is going

5

to get a shock. But they'll like it all right. You see if they don't."

"It's unheard of," protested Carmody. "It's unprecedented."

"There's nothing so pleasant as a healthy change," said Garry. "And listen to this, Greg. That's the sort of thing you're going to get. Because I don't cover any more big sports events unless I go to India."

"Listen, McGowan," hissed Carmody. "That's blackmail. You're the best sports writer in London, and you know it. You're taking unfair advantage of me."

"I'm taking advantage—but I wouldn't call it unfair. I'm doing it in the interests of sportsmanship—and perhaps to a certain extent of Garry McGowan. Would you like me to bring you a little pet elephant from India as a souvenir?"

"All right, you blackmailing scoundrel. You win. Now go and get back that copy."

"Oh no," said Garry. "That particular article stands. Besides, I haven't written anything else, and my public will be disappointed if it doesn't get its Monday morning sporting topic in McGowan's column."

"Of all the unmitigated idiots; of all the impudent, bombastic, cocksure whelps; of all the . . ."

He was still muttering derogatory imprecations when Garry left the office.

Down in the composing-room Jimmy was in a quiet corner engrossed in an avid pre-view of the Monday McGowan article. The colour rose in his cheeks, and he felt the blood thumping through his veins in an ecstasy of excitement. For he read as follows :

> "Yesterday I set out to see a football match, the result of which was the intense interest of every fan in England. Two of the leading teams, composed of some of the cleverest players in the country, were to battle out a vital match.
>
> "As I said, I set out to see this match. On the way I passed a common where some lads of about

14 or 15 years of age had set up impromptu goal-posts and were engaged in a ding-dong struggle. Of science there was little, but of spirit there was plenty. As I passed the ground I idly watched. Then came a brilliant piece of tactical evasive action from a half-back. It really was a grand piece of work. I simply had to stop. Time passed. I was engrossed in the battle royal. Then suddenly I realized I should never get to Wembley in time for the kick-off of the big match. That is a horrible thing for a sports writer to realize. So I decided in a mood of recklessness to let the big match go hang. Instead, I humbly offer my readers the story of the match I saw played between a motley collection of youths who each had one idea and one idea only in his mind—to lick the hide off the other side.

" This was sport—the game for the game's sake, with no reward but bruises and barked shins and the wonderful satisfaction of a game well lost or hardly won. Here was the spirit of sport at its best. And here is the grandest and most exciting game I have seen for a long time, just as I saw it. I offer my apologies to all who look to this column for an account of the big match, but none at all for submitting this story in its stead. . . ."

And Jimmy read Garry McGowan's report of the match in which he himself had captained the side that scored the winning goal in the last tense five minutes of play. He and his pals had ousted the great stars of football from the celebrated McGowan's own column. Jimmy was almost delirious with excitement.

The article proved tremendously popular—if the fan mail it produced was any criterion. Even Carmody grunted grudging approval on the Monday evening when he saw Garry.

" No one yet has dared cover the story of a lot of ragged kids kicking a ball around in place of the biggest match in the country. Only a crazy loon like yourself could do it and get away with it." As he walked away he flung over his shoulder : "Make that Kinchinga story even half as exciting and I'll buy a paper myself, so I will."

CHAPTER V

UNDER WAY

On the voyage to India Garry got to know the other members of the expedition. Dr. Dodd, of course, he had met. Bourne, with his fractured leg, was out of the running, but his nephew had taken his place. When Garry first encountered him at Southampton he recognized his long, loose figure at once. Colin Meighan recognized Garry too, and recalled their previous meeting on the Engadine Express.

Sir Peter explained to Garry : " I think young Meighan is a sound choice. He's as sure and fearless as a chamois on rock. He would make an excellent leader over any difficult rock courses. The only misgiving I have is that I shall have the very deuce of a job to keep a brake on him. He's too impatient and impetuous."

The other members of the party were Mervyn Read, a geologist, and Geoffrey Graham, a botanist.

" While my own particular interest is solely to climb the mountain," Sir Peter explained to Garry, " I realize the value of scientific observation while we are about it. That is why I invited Graham and Read. I know both of them as good climbers. Read was to have gone with one of the Everest parties, but got appendicitis at the crucial moment and had to be ruled out. He's very keen to make up for that disappointment on this trip."

Read was more than fifty, and bald. But he had a ready grin and bright, merry eyes that made him seem extraordinarily youthful. He did not look like a scientist at all, but rather like a farmer or an innkeeper.

Graham, on the other hand, did not look like an open-

air man. The only suggestion of it was in his tanned
skin. Otherwise he looked, in contrast to Read, the
complete student. He was long and thin, with big feet,
and he walked with a sort of loping gait. His shoulders
were narrow and stooped. He had a great mop of hair,
and wore horn-rimmed glasses, through which he frowned
constantly into the far distance. He seemed oblivious
to everyone else. If spoken to, he took some seconds
to bring himself to attention. Then he would smile
slowly and shyly, as though apologizing for his wool-
gathering.

Prior to embarking, Garry had been too busy with
other commissions that Carmody had foisted on him to
probe very deeply into the organization of the expedition.
But once on board ship he had all day to talk things over
with the various members of the party, getting a slant on
their individual jobs as members of a team. He wrote an
article every day, which he radioed to the *Gazette*. With
a couple of hours of strenuous deck-tennis each day as
well, Garry had his time well filled.

The Rawson expedition had by then aroused considerable interest at home. Sir Peter had made a statement
to counter the sneering allegations of a certain section of
the Press. He explained that he had first conceived the
idea of climbing Kinchinga several years before, and had
been carrying out the preliminary organization for many
months. He did not intend to alter his plans one iota
now that an American expedition was in the field. He
had no intention of indulging in a race. At the same
time, he wished luck to the young Americans.

Nevertheless, the prospect of a contest captured public
imagination, and some of the less responsible newspapers
played up the idea with all the enthusiasm of side-show
barkers.

Garry was now giving the more intelligent public some
insight into the work that goes into an attack on a great
mountain peak. Dr. Dodd, for instance, was a medical
man whose special interest was dietetics. As the party
would be away from food sources for perhaps months on

end, it meant that all food would have to be carried by native porters. The porters themselves would eat rice and roughly milled flour. They would have to carry, as well as their own food, the provisions of the white men. The weight they could carry was naturally limited. So Dr. Dodd had spent many months in experiment until he had arrived at a diet plan that would provide a maximum of sustenance with a minimum of weight. That was not nearly so simple as it sounded. Other considerations had to be taken into account as well. In the tropical valleys the food must also have vitamin content that would strengthen the resistance of their bodies to dysentery and cholera, the dread disease that so often ravaged the remote villages in the Himalayan foothills.

Clothes were another subject that called for a great deal of careful thought. It would be extremely cold on the higher levels, with shrieking, cutting blizzards to drive the cold right into the bones. But piles of big woolly overcoats were quite out of the question. Weight was the big consideration—always weight. Clothes had to be light because the heavier they were the less the weight of food and scientific accessories that could be transported. Yet they had to keep their wearers warm in the blizzards and protect them from the sun, whose rays, even in that wilderness of snow and ice, had a tremendous capacity to torture aching bodies. Tents had to be carried to provide shelter when camps were established on the mountain proper. Smaller tents would be used for bivouacs by those who made the final assault. Here, again, the bogy was weight.

These were but some of the problems which very few of the public realized. And Garry now told them the tale :

"Just imagine," he wrote, "your own problems when you go away for a fortnight's holiday. You plan for weeks what you will take and what you will leave. You are lucky if you manage with a single trunkful. And even then you worry because you haven't had room for this or that. You think you ought to take your Harris tweed sports jacket because the nights might be chilly. Yet it will be warm during the day if you get any sun. But you can't take *both* your tweed and your linen jacket ; there won't be room. That is the sort of problem you have to solve. I know. I've done it myself. And we have been going away for only a fortnight, with the weather remaining pretty constant. Next time you're planning your holiday packing, then, just think about planning for a Himalayan expedition, where you not only have your clothes to worry about, but also your bed, roof, and breakfast. And you have to carry all of them on your backs. You aren't going away for two weeks ; you're going away for months. You aren't spending your time by the mild seaside ; you're going through every extreme of climate, from steaming tropical heat to the bitter zero frost of an endless wilderness of snow and ice.

" Think of this. Then you will realize how many months of selecting and rejecting go into the organizing of such an expedition. Only this morning I heard two members of the party arguing as to whether they should or should not take an extra cake of soap. To hear them one would be quite justified in surmising that the argument involved the fate of the whole world. Every half-ounce of weight has an importance beyond measurement."

Colin Meighan was as thrilled about the expedition as a schoolboy who has just got his place in the first eleven. As a matter of fact he was very little more than a schoolboy, being just twenty-one.

" I say, McGowan," he said to Garry one morning as they took a pre-breakfast stroll on the boat-deck. " What do you say to our chances of beating that Yankee party ? "

Garry told him what he knew about the American expedition.

" That's pretty tough," Colin commented afterwards.

" They sound nice kids to me. I hope they manage to do something without actually breaking their necks. But I don't suppose they'll get far."

" My worry is that they'll go too far," Garry told him. " They're as keen as mustard, and they've got all the courage in the world. When they climbed the south face of Mount Macarthur they got badly scared, but they wouldn't give in. Kinchinga isn't Mount Macarthur, and there's no easy way down when you get to the higher altitudes. That's why we've got to get there well before them."

" Sir Peter doesn't seem to be in any hurry," Colin observed.

" He isn't," agreed Garry. " The whole business seems leisurely—like a holiday trip. There isn't the tense atmosphere of excitement that I expected. But I suppose Sir Peter knows best. He wouldn't dawdle for dawdling's sake."

" I feel I want to wade right in," Colin said. " I'm so burnt up inside I feel I could swim there quicker than this tub. When we land I'll want to start running all the way there."

" You go slow, Colin," advised Garry. " Sir Peter won't be pushed, and he won't like it one little bit if you try to hustle him."

The ship's daily news-bulletin gave some attention to the American expedition. Now that Sir Peter had made public his plans, the Mercer crowd had apparently pushed ahead with their plans with feverish haste. Garry had half expected that. They were apparently trying to force a race. That would be to their interest. They could build up a hot story. But it was less to the interest of Larry Elmer and his friends. Garry's insight into the eternal worry and slow accumulation of detail in Sir Peter's organization made it only too apparent how sketchy must be the other party's preparations.

And the greater the haste the greater the danger to which the lads would be exposed. The outcome of the race, of course, was to all knowledgeable people a foregone conclusion. The British party might succeed. The American party by its very nature could not ; and its chances of disaster were far too many. But so far as the Mercer Press was concerned, the principal consideration was that the two attempts should be close enough to suggest a race, and it would whip up public interest to fever pitch. That would mean a tremendous boost in circulation. It was none of its business that the outcome might be tragedy. It made Garry angrier than ever. He wished he could urge Sir Peter into making haste because, if the British party reached the summit, interest would drop completely and the Mercer Press, having nothing further to gain, would probably call the climb off.

The sooner Sir Peter succeeded, then, the less the possibility of the American lads going far enough to get into serious danger. But it was quite certain that he would not jeopardize the lives of his own party and his own chances of success by undue haste and a glossing-over of the seemingly unimportant details. For what may seem trivialities in normal life may well assume gigantic proportions in a blizzard high on a mountain with many days of arduous trudging to the nearest food supply, and that a meagre one.

As Sir Peter once said to Garry : " You know what it's like lying awake with toothache in a comfortable bed in a warm room. Well, imagine lying in a tiny tent on a narrow ledge above a sheer precipice with a blizzard howling outside. You can do nothing but lie there. You may have to wait for days for the storm to blow over. You have scarcely room to move, and you feel half frozen. At high altitudes you have a job to breathe. It makes you horribly depressed. Then you get a bad bout of toothache. Can you imagine it ? It's sometimes hard to put up with in a warm bed. Up there in the mountains it would be enough to drive you almost insane. Then you're glad you remembered to include a pain-killing drug. You see, McGowan, you've got to be prepared for anything."

On arrival at Calcutta the party learned that the American expedition was on the way and was due in about a week's time. Read, who had been up to the Himalayan foothills with the Everest expedition before appendicitis knocked him out, was sent north. He had had some experience of native porters. He struck north-west from Darjeeling by road to the village of Galwal, picking up six Sherpa porters on the way. The Sherpas are renowned as porters. They have intelligence, courage, and fortitude. They are reliable too, in the sense that the climbers know that their Sherpas are doing what they have been told to do. Many Himalayan expeditions have had the disconcerting experience of their porters disappearing without any warning whatever. That is not the sort of thing a Sherpa would do.

Sir Peter never seemed to hurry, yet he never seemed to rest. He was coming and going all day. A constant procession of people visited him at the hotel. Colin Meighan got very impatient.

"Why can't we cut out the parleying and get on with the job?" he demanded of Garry.

"Because Sir Peter wants this picnic to succeed, and, having succeeded, he wants to get back to civilization and not leave his bones or ours on the mountain because someone forgot something," Garry explained.

"Yes, but you've got to be reasonable about it," protested Colin. "Last night he and the Doc argued for an hour about whether they should take a bottle of pills or something for a pain in the tummy or something equally silly."

"I'll bet it was the Doc wanted them."

"It was."

"Who won?"

"The Doc did in the end. But it's so ridiculous arguing about a thing like that."

"You wouldn't think so if you got a bad dose of tummy-ache up there."

"Rot. I haven't had anything like that since I was a kid."

" I'd hold on to myself if I were you," Garry advised.
" You're young and——"

" What about yourself ? "

" Yes, I'm young too. But not so young as you. I'm
old enough to know what Sir Peter and the Doc are about
and I'm prepared to accept their judgment."

A few days later the American party arrived. When
Colin brought Garry the news the latter phoned the local
newspaper to find where the party was staying. That
evening he and Colin went to the rival team's hotel.

Larry Elmer recognized Garry at once. He grinned a
greeting.

" Glad to see you, Mr. McGowan," he said.

" I'm glad to see you, Larry." Garry introduced
Colin. " How do you feel about things, Larry ? "

" I guess we could even climb Everest the way we feel
now." Then his grin faded. " But I mustn't talk to
you about the party. It's exclusive to the Mercer
combine."

" That's all right, Larry," smiled Garry. " Our
policy is to take not a blind bit of notice of you."

Larry bristled. " Is that so ? I s'pose you think we're
not worth considering. We'll show you."

" I've no doubt you'll put up a jolly good show," said
Garry placatingly. " You know I tried to persuade you
against this trip because it was a cheap stunt by a cheap
newspaper."

" Would me and my pals have ever had a chance like
this if it wasn't for that newspaper ? " Larry demanded.

" No, I suppose not," admitted Garry.

" Well, *we're* not complaining. You said they didn't
care what became of us. Well, they aren't sparing
expense or anything. We've even brought an autogyro
with us."

Garry whistled.

" That's a new one," commented Colin. " Climbing
mountains by aeroplane."

" It's for getting our stores and things up into the foothills quickly."

" And you say the Mercer crowd has spared no expense ? " asked Garry.

" Yep. They decided to make a really thorough job of it. They've got a lot of scientific johnnies to work out what stuff we take with us—food and clothes and all that sort of thing."

" H'm," Garry grunted. " They must have got cold feet. Our little bit of publicity did at least have that effect. After what we published in the more serious-minded newspapers there would have been a tremendous outcry if anything had happened to you lads through lack of proper equipment or preparation. That's something. But one word of advice, Larry. This is a dangerous project for comparatively inexperienced climbers. It's better to be a live man who didn't get to the top of a mountain than a dead one who did. Remember that."

" We ain't scared," grinned Larry confidently.

" Which route are you taking ? "

" The Mercer Press got some guy who used to live up near the Himalayas to work out a route. We're being flown up to a valley in the foothills. It's about 8000 feet up. It's a sort of flat, grassy place. This guy has come with us. He knows where it is. He reckons a gyroplane could easily land and take off there. Then he'll put us on the way. It's up a gorge ; that's all I know about it."

" The Banghiri Gorge, I expect," suggested Colin.

" Some name like that, anyway," said Larry.

" Well, that's stealing a march, if you like ! " gasped Colin. " Sir Peter turned that route down because it meant such a long trek by a hard, slow trail to get to the gorge. We would have used so much extra food and energy before we got to the real jumping-off place. Now they're using a gyro to get there. It isn't fair."

Larry smiled triumphantly.

" It's fair enough," pondered Garry. " Once you start climbing mountains with artificial aids it's hard to say where to draw the line. We're taking pitons and ropes and things, aren't we ? They're artificial aids. No, if they can get a gyro up there it's fair enough. The mountain proper is that huge cone that towers up 8000 feet from every surrounding ridge. These fellows will still have a hard 9000 feet to climb before they get to Kinchinga itself. After all, the idea is to climb Kinchinga, not the mountains that cluster round its base."

" I say, it sounds as if you're going over to the enemy," complained Colin.

" Not at all. Credit where credit is due ; an open mind, and all that sort of thing."

" Which way is your crowd going ? " asked Larry.

" The East Ridge," replied Colin. " Sir Peter says there's some very stiff rock-climbing on exposed faces, but it's a route that's pretty well protected from the weather."

" What are you doing about porters ? " asked Garry.

" The guy who has lived here is arranging that for us. He's been in the district so long he almost looks like one of those Chinky little bozos."

" They're not Chinks exactly," corrected Garry.

" They look like them. So what's the difference ? You know the little guys I mean."

" Yes, I know," said Garry.

" Look here, Garry," said Colin a little pettishly, " I thought you said this expedition was phoney ? It seems to me they've made a pretty thorough job of things."

Garry shrugged and grinned.

" It seems so," he said. " They've changed their minds somewhat. That's because after promoting this stunt they'd look pretty foolish if Sir Peter succeeded and they failed miserably. And in the event of tragedy, which God forbid, any suggestion of slapdash methods would do the Mercer Press an awful lot of harm."

" Then you think this expedition has some chance of success ? "

" It's a possibility. If inexperience doesn't lead Larry and his pals into trouble, and they have reasonable luck, I don't see why it shouldn't be a possibility."

" We can look after ourselves all right," reassured Larry Elmer.

Colin seemed taken aback.

" You're not scared ? " Garry asked him. " What's wrong with a properly organized expedition as a rival ? I know you're pretty keen on the idea of being first on the summit of Kinchinga. But a little healthy competition will do no harm."

" That means a real race ? " said Colin.

" It seems rather likely. Except that I don't imagine Sir Peter will speed up his plans or let the fact of a properly organized rival expedition influence him in the slightest degree."

" But he's got to," protested Colin. " Now it's a case of British prestige and all that."

Garry grinned. " May the best men win."

" If these chaps win, the Mercer Press won't half have the laugh on us."

" Well, I'm forgetting the Mercer Press for the time being," said Garry. " I'll think about them later. All I'm going to worry about for the present is the conquest of Kinchinga. If these lads have got it in them to win out, then I wish them luck, Mercer Press or no Mercer Press."

" You scoundrel, McGowan," spluttered Colin. " I believe you're hugging yourself that it's going to be a race."

" As a sporting journalist I can't deny that the prospect gives me a lot of pleasure."

" I thought that you weren't going to mention us in your newspapers," chuckled Larry Elmer.

Garry glanced sideways at Colin and loosened his collar.

" It looks as though I'll have to do a little climbing down," he admitted. " I hate climbing down. But I've got to give credit where credit is due. Whatever the motives of the Mercer combine, they are at least making this a serious attempt on the mountain now. And I've got to own up to it."

The door opened and Kell entered, accompanied by two young men whom Garry knew to be the other members of the party.

" Ah, the great and glorious McGowan ! " chirped Kell. " I thought I might run across you here in India. Doing a little snooping ? "

" This was intended to be a friendly visit," said Garry. " So far it has been. I should like it to go on being one for the sake of all concerned. I have no intention whatever of probing your precious exclusive rights."

Larry introduced his friends, Ted Cray and Tex Butcher. They were of a kind with Larry—long, sinewy slabs of youngsters, with a lot of open air in their faces and rather shy eyes, as though overcome by the fact that they, a couple of ordinary young Americans living quiet unpretentious lives, were now basking in the unrelenting glare of the spotlight of world attention. Garry and Colin shook hands with all three youths and wished them luck as they took their leave. Kell could not refrain from one parting, nasty crack.

" Must you be going ? Yes, of course you must. You must run along and tell your Lord Peter or whatever his name is that he'd better put on his running spikes, because it isn't a phoney expedition he's up against after all."

Garry did not answer.

" One of these days I'll show that slicker how I feel about him," he muttered to Colin as he closed the door. " And he'll be sorry he didn't take ten easy lessons from Joe Louis."

" I don't like him," said Colin. " He's the sort of chap you don't take to. ' I do not like thee, Mr. Kell, the reason why I cannot tell ; but this I know, and know full well, I do not like thee, Mr. Kell.' "

Garry laughed at Colin's paraphrase of the well-known quip.

" But I like those young Yanks," Colin went on. " They're nice blokes. They're different from us—sort of easier going, more natural. They seem to think climbing this mountain is one deuce of a fine picnic. It's the way I feel about it myself. But when you get chaps like the Doc and Sir Peter going into all that dull organizing business you feel it's taking all the kick and thrill out of it. We've been here a week, talking and arguing, and I haven't seen even a respectable hill, let alone a mountain."

" You'll see all you want before you've finished," promised Garry.

" I wish those Yanks didn't have to rely on that cheap stunt idea," Colin said, after a few moments of thoughtful frowning.

" I know," sighed Garry. " I don't hold any brief for the Mercer crowd or their motives. I hate to see those lads being shepherded by a fellow like Kell. But so far as the lads are concerned, as ordinary human youngsters, it's a wonderful chance. So, as I said, I'm going to forget all about the Mercer crowd so long as they play the game from now on. But any cheap tricks on Kell's part and I go on the rampage."

Garry rather thought that Colin would try to urge Sir Peter to hasten. As they sat at supper later that night he could not help but notice how Colin's demeanour suggested that his chair was stuffed with tin-tacks. The Doc and Sir Peter were involved in one of their interminable arguments about what should and what should not be included in equipment. Graham, the long, lean, absent-minded botanist, consumed his meal with such concentration that it seemed eating was the greatest interest he had. Neither Colin nor Garry had so far succeeded in penetrating the shell of his absent-mindedness. Read, who had returned south after settling arrangements about porterage, ate instinctively while he read a book on geology. It was impolite, no doubt, but they had become accustomed to his habit of taking every meal to the accompaniment of the recorded knowledge of science. The members of the expedition always ate together, and for Colin and Garry, as the junior members of the party, meals were pretty stodgy affairs.

At last Colin could contain himself no longer.

" I say," he said, " McGowan and I have been over to see the American crowd."

" American crowd ? " Sir Peter repeated questioningly.

" The American expedition."

" Oh, the American expedition ! . . . As—a—I was saying, Dodd, the question of the effect of pure oxygen on the blood corpuscles . . ."

Garry grinned wryly at Colin and shook his head, but Colin was not to be discouraged.

" I say," he tried again, " we were mistaken about them, you know. We thought they were phoney."

" Phoney ? " queried the Doc, not understanding.

" American for fake, superficial, or cheap," Garry recited for his information.

" Well, they're not," Colin continued. " They've gone into things pretty thoroughly. McGowan and I have come to the conclusion that they are to be considered quite seriously as rivals. If we don't shake ourselves up we might be beaten to Kinchinga."

Sir Peter turned from the Doc and looked at Colin some time before speaking. " I am not the least interested in the American expedition. I am interested only in climbing this mountain. I dislike being urged. You understand ? "

Colin gulped uncomfortably.

Graham came suddenly to life. " If we hurry," he said, " I should have little time for studying botanical specimens in the foothills. I am extremely anxious to find new species of *Paratori lugubrii*."

Colin glared at the botanist.

" But a race would be most exciting," Graham went on after a moment's thought. " I could no doubt do my collecting on the return trip."

Colin smiled delight. The dreamy scientist had suddenly become human. Read, too, forgot his book for the moment and became absorbed in the prospect.

" I say," he said, " what an experience it would be ! Remember the race to conquer the Matterhorn ? This would be much more exciting than that. It's on a so much bigger scale."

6

Sir Peter frowned.

" I find this preoccupation with the idea of a race irritating.   Once and for all, this expedition will not deviate from its set course."

There was a deep, brittle silence for some moments. Then Sir Peter resumed his conversation with the Doc.

After supper Colin and Garry retired to a corner of the lounge.

" Is Sir Peter human ? " demanded Colin in exasperation.

" I've usually found him so."

" But he can't be.   Any human being couldn't help being excited at the prospect of a race like that.   Garry, you can talk the legs off a dozen iron pots.   Can't you persuade him ? "

" Not on your life.   Sir Peter is absolutely set in this matter, and dynamite wouldn't blow him off his course."

A few days later Garry and Colin took a taxi to the aerodrome where the Americans' autogyro was being assembled.   Larry and his friends Tex and Ted were there too.   They viewed the shining new machine with unconcealed admiration and excitement.   It gave Garry some pleasure just to watch them.   For these three lads a story-book adventure was to become an actual fact.

Larry introduced Graeme Green, the " guy who used to live in the Himalayas."   Garry liked the man. He was about fifty, with a gaunt, leathery face that surprisingly broke into a grin on the slightest provocation. Green volunteered the information that his profession was a rolling-stone.   He knocked about the world picking up jobs as they came—if they were exciting or interesting enough.   He was the sort of man who, had he lived in another age, might have discovered the Pacific or America or Australia or the North-West Passage.   But he lived in a world which had been fully discovered, and that fact was the only regret of his life.

" You don't talk like an American," Garry commented.

" No," said Green.   " I was in America when I heard

about this newspaper gang wanting a guy who knew a bit about the Himalayas. As a matter of fact I was born in England—Durham. But I took my first job at fifteen —in a boat. And I've knocked around so much since I hardly think of myself as having any nationality. I guess I just belong to the old world, and I feel the world kinda belongs to me. Boy, it's a grand feeling."

" Are you going with the lads ? " Colin asked.

" Me ? " grunted Green. " Not on your life. I don't mind going up in aeroplanes, but I don't take kindly to the idea of turning human fly and crawling up perpendicular mountains. No, sir, heights make me come over funny. Climbing is about the one exciting thing I never took to. Once I thought I'd like to follow up this Monster of Kinchinga tale and——"

" The Monster of Kinchinga ? " broke in Colin. " Is there anything to that yarn ? "

" Heaven knows. I never got the strong of it. The natives swear black, blue, and blind about it. But they're funny coves. They've got so many other queer notions you hardly know what to believe. I never found out for myself because I got no further than the alps this side of the Banghiri Gorge. There wasn't much climbing to get that far—just a lot of hard foot-slogging. After that, you come to real mountain-climbing. And that's where yours truly leaves off."

" What is the monster supposed to be like ? "

" I've never heard two natives who say they saw it ever say the same thing. I guess it's bad dreams. They say it's a sort of king of the mountain and kills anyone who goes on to its preserves. You'd never get the local natives on to the mountain for love or money. That's why all the porters have got to come from other parts. They won't mind going up any mountain if you pay them enough—and it doesn't have to be much by our standards. But a million dollars wouldn't kid *me* on to it. No, sir, all my job with this outfit is to guide the younkers to the alps by the Banghiri Gorge—that means I show Kell where they are, flying up there in the gyro ; and I also get the porters for them. I know something of the native lingo, so I'm a sort of liaison officer as well."

" Is Kell piloting the plane ? " Garry asked.

" Yes. He's done a bit of flying in the States. Is he a friend of yours ? "

" Well, I wouldn't go so far as to say that," answered Garry.

" H'm," grunted Green. " So far as that goes, I can't imagine him being a friend of anybody. He's got a way of rubbing people up the wrong way. If he doesn't watch himself with the porters he'll find trouble. They're queer cusses—take delicate handling. If Kell tries the tactics he uses on the Indian servants at the hotel he'll find bother, and plenty of it."

" Does that mean Kell is going with the lads ? " Colin asked.

" He's talking about going as far as the base camp and taking a portable radio transmitter. But I guess he'll get scared before he gets half-way up the first precipice."

" I wouldn't swear to that," chipped in Larry Elmer. " I don't like the guy myself ; but what I've seen of him, I wouldn't say he was a funk."

Garry and Colin hoped to meet Green later. He was the sort of man anyone would like to meet again.

That evening at supper Sir Peter announced that on the morrow the party would be leaving for Darjeeling, whence they would strike out through the outlying villages to the foot of the mighty Kinchinga.

Colin's face glowed with the prospect of action at last. Garry half expected him to cheer very loudly. He wanted to cheer himself.

The party was glad to get to Darjeeling for more reasons than one. In Calcutta the air had been particularly humid, and movement had been an effort. In Darjeeling it was dry and invigorating, and after the heat of the plains the men felt they wanted to run and leap simply because movement seemed so pleasantly effortless. Or perhaps it was the sudden contrast in climates that made them feel that way. For Garry and Colin, who had not been there before, there was the great moment when they saw the Himalayas for the first time—the distant snow-capped peaks above clouds ; and so white and wispy did they appear that it was difficult at first to distinguish them from the clouds. It was only by observing the slow swirl of mist that the giants, by their immobility, were discerned. Neither of the young men could quite believe they were real—so majestic, so remote, so entirely removed from the world of men did they seem.

Sometimes they had the ethereal unreality of a dreamed fairyland. At other times, when their mood changed, and the sun floodlit them from low in the sky as through a rose gelatine, they had the hard unreality of a painted theatrical backcloth. Kinchinga, tucked away in that wilderness of snow and ice, was not visible from here.

The party were in Darjeeling for two days only. Arrangements had been practically completed in Calcutta, and Sir Peter and the Doc—the brains of the expedition —were satisfied that down to the last-minute detail the organization was as complete as human ingenuity could make it.

It soon became apparent to the others that Sir Peter would not want to stay long in Darjeeling. For their hotel was full of people resting and enjoying a respite from the heat of the plains. These people had little to occupy their minds but tennis and bridge and dancing —all occupations which are quickly dulled by repetition —unless one is lucky enough to be an expert. So the arrival of a Himalayan expedition was a welcome break in the monotony, and the members of the party were pestered by swarms of the idly curious who displayed considerable ingenuity in the production of idiotic questions.

Garry and Colin, who had little to do with the actual organization, were appalled by the packing-cases which they saw being loaded on to the motor trucks. It seemed incredible that so much gear could be carried into the mountains on the backs of men. The journey to Kalmet

was hazardous, and none of the men could honestly admit
to enjoying it. The road from Darjeeling to Kalmet was
long, rough, and dangerous. At times it crawled round
the edges of hills which anywhere else in the world but
here, where they are dwarfed by the Himalayan giants,
would be called mountains. The road was narrow, too,
and at every bend it seemed that the trucks must take off
and shoot into space ; but somehow they slithered round
the corners safely. The native drivers grinned happily,
proud of their prowess, and seemingly utterly ignorant
of the law of gravity.

At Kalmet the porters were waiting and the party
made the acquaintance of Kipar, the head porter—a
Sherpa man. There were six Sherpa men altogether, and
about thirty men from Kalmet itself. These latter were
the donkey workers of the expedition. Their job was to
carry the equipment to the base camp in the foothills
below the mountain. They were strong physically but,
unlike the Sherpas, were undeveloped mentally. On the
lower levels, where no particular courage or initiative
or intelligence was required, they would be adequate.
These men would be dismissed at the base camp and the
Sherpas, intelligent and used to climbing, would carry
the necessary equipment on to the mountain itself. Then
the Sherpas in turn would be left, and the Europeans
would themselves carry their gear to the highest levels.
And perhaps only two or three of them would actually
reach the summit.

Garry attempted to describe for his readers the system
behind the organization by suggesting that the expedition
could be likened to a space rocket. The expedition, as
also the rocket, could only progress by power. When a
motor-car runs short of petrol—or power—it can stop at
the next roadside garage. But a rocket going into sterile
space and an expedition penetrating a wild and unfruitful
country have to take their own power. With the rocket
the power is the explosive charge ; with the expedition,
food. In all progress the power is consumed. People
who dream of space travel design their rockets with many

chambers to contain the propelling charges. When one chamber is exhausted, and thus becomes a dead and useless weight to be pulled along, it is uncoupled and falls off, and the next chamber takes up the propulsion until ultimately only the head of the rocket, a very small part of the apparatus originally discharged, remains. But the head is the important part, and its arrival the object of the whole apparatus. So it was with the expedition. The propulsion chambers—or porters—would be dropped off as they progressed. The farther the party travelled the less food and equipment would remain, and so porters could be dispensed with. Indeed they would only be dead weight as they went on. Needless to say, the party had also to bear in mind the return journey, which also consumes power.

In expeditions striving to conquer Himalayan peaks sometimes scores of men set out carrying tons of equipment, and only two or three men with a few pounds of the bare necessities of life slung on their backs in rucksacks actually achieve the absolute peak. They are the head of the rocket ; the remainder are the propulsion chambers.

Kalmet, the climbers found, was a little stony village sprawling over the side of a steep hill. It centred round a Buddhist temple—a garish, vividly painted little building that would probably look very fine in photographs but in actual fact looked shabby and dirty and stank of a nauseating staleness. The villagers, too, would no doubt look romantic and colourful in photographs, but they also looked shabby and dirty when seen with the eyes of reality ; and it must be added they also smelled rank. They took a poor view of water for any purpose but drinking.

In all that ancient village there was but one touch of modernity—a rusty-looking petrol pump. It stood forlorn, a lone sentinel on the last outpost of communication with civilization. Here the road, such as it was, ended. The trucks were unloaded. From here the attack on Kinchinga really began. The mountain was still hidden away, and its summit was about thirty miles as the crow flies from Kalmet.

Colin waxed impatient again as the cases were unpacked and the food and equipment sorted and loaded into packs. The packs were then assigned to their appropriate porters. Both Garry and Colin, the rookies of the party, were amazed at the size and weight of the packs. But the porters accepted their burdens with no sign of dismay on their complacent oriental faces. The distribution took two days. The slow stupidity of the Kalmet men exasperated Colin, who was chafing to be off. These men had very little comprehension of their duties. Nor did Kipar's angry voice and loud threats and free use of a vicious-looking stick succeed in drumming sense into them. Sir Peter, however, accepted the whole business with a philosophical patience. The native stupidity of porters, so far as he was concerned, was just another obstacle ; and mountaineering, when all is said and done, is merely a matter of overcoming obstacles—mostly solid, perpendicular ones.

But at length the preparations were complete, and in the chill darkness of one early morning Garry and Colin found themselves being unceremoniously shaken out of their camp beds. Coldly and uncomfortably they dressed and went from their tent to see figures moving vaguely in the grey dawn. There were low, complaining voices. The jargon was completely unintelligible, but there was no mistaking the feelings of the Kalmet men. They were at least human enough to resent—as do all right-thinking men—the misery of turning out of warm bunks on bitterly cold and dark mornings. Kipar's strident voice could be heard above the moaning. Occasionally, too, could be heard the thwack of his stick, always followed by a howl of pain.

Order somehow emerged from chaos, and at last a long line of heavily laden men moved off in single file, their faces towards the mountains, whose topmost peaks were just beginning to glow with the roseate glory of dawn.

The great adventure had truly begun at last.

A LONG LINE OF HEAVILY LADEN MEN MOVED OFF IN SINGLE FILE.

CHAPTER VI

ONWARD AND UPWARD

AFTER the first high excitement of being on the move, the mood of the party flattened. The start was, after all, the glorious promise, but before they achieved the majesty of the mountains there would be a terrific amount of drudgery and dull trekking. The older men, being wise in years, were patient ; but Garry and Colin felt a growing urge to hustle the pace. The porters, after each stop, spent so much time getting their packs on, adjusting them and jostling leisurely into line, that Garry bemoaned the fact that military training of the good old jump-to-it school was not a feature of life in Kalmet.

" If you could only shout at them : ' Squad, fall in. 'Shun. Right turn. Quick march ! ' " he wished pathetically.

The route lay along a valley. On either side hills soared steeply, their slopes rank with dense vegetation. Along the floor of the valley a river raged and roared. Here it was a broad, swift, shallow stream, and there a narrow, boiling torrent that would destroy any living thing that ventured into it. There was no road, so the Europeans had to do a considerable amount of pioneering work. Often it became necessary to cross from one side of the river to the other ; they would find the going steepening until there was no foot-hold at all and the base of the hill reared into a cliff. Then they would have to retrace their steps, cross the river where its violence was comparatively lulled, and continue on the opposite side. Each mile seemed appallingly long and slow in the covering. The heat was a great factor. It was a steamy heat that sucked the energy out of limbs, and made one dream of sitting on mossy green banks beside cool, tranquil streams instead of trudging over rough, dusty ways beneath a shrivelling sun.

All the time the American expedition, too, was heading slowly towards Kinchinga.

On the southern side Kinchinga breaks into three long ridges, not unlike the prongs of a fork. Between the ridges lie two deep valleys. The easterly one was the one that Sir Peter's party was following. It would ultimately lead them to the steep wall in which both these valleys ended. Before they reached that, however, they would strike up on to the ridge. As soon as they got above the tree-line the ridge would provide reasonable going. At lower levels its dense vegetation would hamper progress and much energy would be needlessly wasted in going up and down its myriad hills which, from a distance, looked like the temperature chart of a patient who couldn't make up his mind whether to be sick or well.

The American party was following the western valley up to the Banghiri Gorge. That route was much longer, but the use of the autogyro would put the party well on their way and save them the long, wearisome journey. That route had the advantage of a shorter distance to the summit once the bulk of Kinchinga itself had been achieved. On the other hand, it was a more exposed route and likely to be much more affected by the vagaries of the weather.

Thus the two parties wended their respective ways, each following a valley and each separated from the other by the centre ridge—a broad buttress soaring 4000 feet above the floors of the valleys. In effect, the routes of the two parties were sometimes no more than five miles apart.

Both parties carried portable radio transmitters and receivers. It was the only possible contact with the civilized world. So far as Sir Peter was concerned, the radio was unnecessary. He was prepared, for many weeks, to live on his wits and his resources. But Garry, as a journalist, had to get his copy to press. So each day, as the party penetrated farther and farther into the mountain fastnesses, he sent out his progress report. It was received in Darjeeling and then cabled to London.

Thus the suburban householder journeying to his own dull routine job read all about it a few hours after Garry had sent it.

The radio also enabled Sir Peter's party to keep in touch with worldly happenings. They were able to follow the movements of the American party, too, for Kell was radioing his reports to his own representative in Darjeeling. Kell's was a very exclusive report. It was radioed on to New York, where the Mercer Press released a version of the story to agencies for publication outside the United States, they themselves retaining the sole American rights. The agencies distributed the story throughout the world for Press and radio publication. So it was that, after the report had gone all the way to America and back, Garry could follow the movements of the American party, which was, in fact, never more than a mere twenty miles away from him.

Garry carried a map of the terrain. It was not a very good map. The Himalayan wilderness is not charted with the minute detail of an Ordnance Survey map of the North Wales mountains, for instance. Few white men penetrate the Himalayan hinterland, and surveying is mostly a matter of long-distance observation from scattered points. However, Garry was able to pencil in the progress of the rival parties with reasonable accuracy.

Colin's impatience grew. The Europeans carried only rucksacks containing special instruments and personal equipment. The porters were very heavily laden with packages that often seemed larger than the men themselves. Thus while the porters plodded slowly along, the white men could move with comparative agility. They often moved forward, surveying the route well in advance. If the porters started upon a section which proved to be impassable the retreat was slow, whereas if the impassability were discovered before the porters reached it no progress was lost.

Colin in his impatience often pushed on far ahead on his own, and several times, finding the party not overtaking him, had to wend his way back, usually to find it pitching camp. This exasperated him. Nevertheless, after a few days the pencil lines on Garry's map showed appreciable progress.

Meanwhile the party learnt by radio that the American party had successfully transferred its equipment and climbers to the meadows, or alps, above the Banghiri Gorge by means of the gyroplane. There they had made rendezvous with the native porters who had been rounded up and conducted thence by Graeme Green. The rival party was therefore a jump ahead. It was at least fifteen miles nearer Kinchinga than Sir Peter's party— not that miles meant the same thing there as they did on Salisbury Plain, for instance. Each mile had to be picked out carefully over rough and sometimes treacherous routes. Sometimes a mile would involve a climb of 2000 feet or more. That is hard going enough on a smooth road without an overwhelming pack on the back. So it was impossible to estimate the real advantage in start that the gyro had given the American lads. Nevertheless it must have been considerable.

" I don't call that playing the game," Colin complained.

" Why not ? " demanded Garry.

" You're supposed to climb the mountain, not fly on to it."

" They're not flying on to it, Colin. They're merely using a superior propulsion chamber in part of their rocket. After all, you've got to use some mechanical aids in climbing a mountain like Kinchinga, and where you draw the line is your own affair. If we were purists in the matter we would have swum from London to Calcutta and walked from Calcutta to Kalmet. Instead we went by steamer to Calcutta, by air to Darjeeling, and to Kalmet by motor truck."

" Well, I'd sooner have walked than gone in that rackety motor truck with its stark crazy driver ! " retorted Colin.

The days went by and Garry's pencilled position lines lengthened. Yet they could not draw up on the Americans. Colin took to assisting Kipar in urging on the porters to ever more speed. He shouted at them and made frantic gestures at them, but to no avail. They stared at him blankly and uncomprehendingly. Plain English was useless. He did achieve some little success, however, by roaring at them a meaningless string of Biblical names. " Jeremiah, Ezekiel, Nebuchadnezzar, Nehemiah, Apocalypse ! " uttered in a vicious, clipped voice was particularly impressive and efficacious. Such language must mean something dire, decided the Kalmet men, and hurried their pace—but only while Colin's eye was on them. On the whole, however, any attempt at speeding up was unavailing, and the older men got a great deal of amusement out of Colin's efforts.

In his efforts to urge the party to greater speed Colin pushed too far ahead alone on one occasion. There was some misunderstanding as to his intentions. The route he followed seemed clear enough. He halted, and waited to make sure that the party was following. By late afternoon they had not arrived, and he began to retrace his steps. Then the dramatically sudden tropical night overtook him, and he was obliged to bivouac in a most uncomfortable crevice.

The following morning he hastened back and found Read and Garry at a ford to which they had come in search of him. They were not a little worried, and impressed him pretty forcibly with the poor view they took of his pioneering. At the ford the valley forked. One fork was a narrow, unpromising-looking ravine, the other a broad and obvious passage. But Colin had been too careless in the reading of his map. The broad valley ended a few miles farther on in a blank mountainside. The narrow gorge, which later widened again, was the gully that ran up to the foot of Kinchinga.

So a chastened and shamefaced Colin accompanied Garry and Read to where the main party waited. His impatience had cost half a day's march. That apparently did not worry Sir Peter. Nor did it worry Graham, the botanist, who had seized the opportunity for an excursion into the wooded slopes in search of botanical specimens.

When Colin arrived Graham was missing, and a general scout around, accompanied by much shouting, ensued. It was an hour before he was located and the party on the move again. After that episode Colin curbed his impatience.

The country got more and more rugged and the going slower. The daily progress lines on the map got shorter and shorter. That also went for the American party. Then, in another few days, the British party drew level with the Americans, who seemed to have come to a standstill. The radio reports emanating from the Americans gave little information. They merely stated that progress had become difficult. Garry could not understand it. On his map the positions of the two parties seemed to be only five miles apart. Garry drew Colin's attention to the fact.

" Let's make a friendly call on them," Garry suggested.

" Not on your life," retorted Colin. " We've got to win this race."

" We could make it easily enough," Garry said. " To-morrow we face the ledges that Sir Peter has christened the Mappin Terraces. There's nearly 3000 feet of climbing in them. It will take the porters all day to negotiate them, because the going is rough and with their huge loads they can't climb with the same ease as an unladen man. We could get across to the Banghiri Gorge and back easily in a day."

" All right," agreed Colin. " We'll see what Sir Peter says."

The two went to Sir Peter's tent.

" You may as well go," the leader said. " There won't be much you can do. The Kalmet men will have to be nursed up the Mappin Terraces. I think the Sherpas, who know a little about mountaineering, are the best men for that job. You'd only start your Biblical barracking, Colin, and we'd have the porters tumbling down the terraces in sheer fright."

Early the following morning Garry and Colin put food in rucksacks, filled water bottles, and struck up across the vast buttress, rising to 4000 feet above the floor of the valley. At this height vegetation was sparse, and most of the climb was of a scrambling nature. Only twice did they find it advisable to rope up. On these occasions Colin led and instructed Garry as to how to move. Inexperienced climber though he was, Garry did not find the traverses across the exposed faces particularly difficult. Certainly the sight of the awful chasm below was something of a trial for the nerves ; but Garry had at various times during his life driven cars at better than 100 m.p.h., and had twice baled out of aeroplanes which had cracked up under his rigorous handling in test flights. Those things, he reflected, were much more dangerous. After all, if you have a good hand-hold why worry about falling, even if the drop is a perpendicular half-mile ? Two thousand feet or two hundred feet—or even twenty feet—if you fell the result could be the same in all cases.

The last 1500 feet of the climb was in snow. Many times the climbers thought that the summit ridge was in sight, only to find when they achieved it that yet another ridge of snow-topped rock lay above them. But at last the skyline dropped away and before them appeared a wonderful spectacle. Mile upon mile of mountain wastes lay about them. In the valley the steep slopes had shut out practically all view. Now a chaotic tumble of snow-clad giants gleamed peacefully in the sun ; and above them one soared superb—the queen of all. Both men at once recognized the contours from photographs they had seen. They did not need to remark the beauty and the majesty of their first sight of Kinchinga. Their blood chilled with the immense thrill of it. The pyramid from whose summit the snow streamed like blown spume from a rearing wave was the goal of their every activity for the past month. So peaceful it looked. Yet both knew that on the serene-looking top even at that moment there was raging an unimaginable storm.

Colin looked at Garry. He raised his eyebrows, and grinned slightly.

" Well, that's it," he said.

That was all. They turned their backs on the spectacle and tramped across the snowy plateau. The plateau began to slope steeply into another valley, the opposite wall of which they could see soaring into yet another ridge. The floor of the valley could not be seen until the slope became steeper still. It lay nearly a mile below. Somewhere in its depths was the American expedition.

The descent was fairly easy. Although steep, the rock was well broken into safe ledges. Half-way down, Garry and Colin halted. They brought binoculars to bear on the scene and slowly scanned the length of the gorge.

" I see them," Garry shouted suddenly, and pointed.

Colin, after some moments, spotted them too. In such vastness a party of mere men is not easy to espy.

" But what's wrong ? " Colin asked. " Their tents are still pitched. At this hour they ought to be well on the move."

" It is peculiar," Garry grunted.

The two men pushed on, and within an hour were approaching the American encampment. They did not see the lads. Some native porters squatted around their fires smoking cheap cigarettes and quarrelling among themselves.

Garry hailed.

A fair, tousled head appeared from a tent. It was Larry Elmer's. Larry's face creased into an incredulous grin. Then he whooped.

" Says, fellers, we've got visitors."

His two companions quickly followed him out of the tent, and a moment later a great deal of hand-pumping was going on.

" What's the idea ? " Larry demanded. " You haven't come over to the enemy ? "

" Nothing like," Garry told him. " We worked out that we weren't a million miles away from you so we dropped over the fence, so to speak. How's everything ? "

Larry's grin slid straight.

7

" As a matter of fact we've struck a spot of bother,"
he said. " Trouble with the porters."

Colin and Garry exchanged glances.

" Then that's why you haven't moved these last few
days ? " Colin asked.

" I guess so."

" What sort of trouble ? " Garry asked.

" Well, they didn't like being pushed. Kell kept on
trying to hustle the pace. The headman guy—well, he
was all right. He used to kick the others along a bit.
But they still didn't go fast enough for Kell, so he started
kicking them along himself. They sort of take it from
one of their own guys, but they didn't like it from a white
man. One turned on Kell and dropped his load and
told him what he thought of him. You couldn't make
out a word he said, of course ; but gee ! he sure sounded
sore. Kell shouted at him : ' You dirty Chinks won't
answer me back,' and he took a stick and gave the poor
creature the mother and father of a thrashing." Larry
pointed to a porter who sat apart from the rest, a brooding
mask on his impassive face. " That's the one."

" What next ? " asked Garry.

" The next morning there were just a lot of bundles
and one headman in the camp. The others had all
scrammed. So Kell took his gun and cleared off down
the gorge after them. He caught up with them all right.
They might have been nasty about it, too, only Kell
pointed to the gun and then knocked off an eagle that
came a bit too low, probably to see what it was all about.
Then he pointed the gun at them. I guess that did the
trick. They came back pronto."

" Where's Kell now ? " Garry asked.

" Gone looking for Green. A few days ago Tex went
scouting ahead, and just above where that waterfall is "
—he pointed it out—" he found there's a grassy clearing.
It's just at the foot of where Kinchinga really starts.
Kell figured if he could lift the gyroplane high enough
to land it there it would mean he could get back to
civilization quicker when the stunt's finished. I shouldn't

be surprised if he doesn't think it might be handy for a getaway too. He's scared stiff of those porter guys. And Mister Kell ain't Number One Popular Man around these parts. So he's gone back to the alp where we left Green with the gyro. We're waiting to see if he makes it. If he isn't back by to-morrow, we go on."

Almost on top of Larry's words a low droning sound throbbed distantly above the chatter of the swift nearby stream.

" I thought I heard the plane," said Ted.

" So did I," said Colin.

They turned and looked down the gorge. Against the sky, which showed like a theatre backdrop between the flanking walls of the gorge, something flashed in the sun. It was the whirling rotor of the gyro. Slowly it approached, the nose pointed upwards in an effort to make every inch of altitude. A gyroplane cannot reach anywhere near the altitude of a high-powered winged plane equipped with variable-pitch air-screw. Its ceiling is comparatively low. Although neither party of climbers had yet reached the mountain itself, they had already achieved a considerable height, and it seemed a hazardous business for a gyro to attempt such a flight. Not only was the country wild and rugged in the extreme, but the gyro could not fly high enough to get out of trouble in an emergency. It was coming up the gorge now at the maximum height it could attain in that rarefied atmosphere.

Garry, not being unused to aircraft, guessed that fact from the sound of the labouring engine. On either side the gorge walls soared thousands of feet above the floor. At the height the gyro was flying the walls were barely a hundred and fifty yards apart. One hundred and fifty yards was scarcely a lot of space for an aeroplane to play around in. Despite Garry's feelings for Kell, he could not restrain a certain admiration for the man's cool nerve.

The porters crouched, and watched the plane in abject fear. Garry felt sorry for them. It was obvious that the white man's magic reduced them to terror. It was not right, Garry thought, that these men should be bullied by their fear of civilized machinery. He spoke to them :

"It's all right," he said. "Nothing to get scared about."

He knew that they could not understand him, but he hoped his tone of voice would convey assurance. It did not. Garry shrugged helplessly. Colin grinned at him and winked. He walked over and addressed himself to the natives. His face was solemn and he intoned slowly, in a deep, smooth voice, his Biblical catalogue. The natives listened fascinated. With much gesture of pointing to the plane, pointing to the porters, and holding his hand to his heart, Colin pursued his meaningless lecture. He beamed at them with all the affection of a fond uncle surveying his brood of nephews. It worked. The natives were reassured. Slow grins drove fear from their eyes.

"Now what price old Nebuchadnezzar?" Colin demanded.

"You mean that wasn't language at all?" asked Larry.

"Quite, quite without rhyme or reason," Colin replied.

"Well, I'll hike to Hong Kong!" exclaimed Larry in unconcealed admiration.

The gyroplane passed slowly over them at a height of less than two hundred feet. The watchers on the ground could see that there was someone else beside the pilot in the plane. Almost simultaneously two arms appeared over the side of the cockpit and two tiny parachutes made from pocket-handkerchiefs were left floating in the air behind the machine and descending slowly. Colin got one, Larry Elmer the other. Each had a message attached.

Larry Elmer read his : "Have brought Graeme Green with me. I don't get the hang of these natives. Maybe he can do better. LOUIS KELL."

"What's the other one say?" asked Garry.

Colin had already opened it. He read : " This guy is stark crazy. If anything happens, send all my worldly belongings to my brother, P. Green, 1096 Whitehorse Road, Box Hill, Melbourne, Australia. *Signed*, GRAEME GREEN. P.S.—I'll never go in an aeroplane again. P.P.S.—I probably won't have another chance anyway."

The others laughed loudly at the queer last will and testament. It was natural to laugh at someone else's discomfort, but they could nevertheless appreciate Green's feelings. Kell was obviously a skilled pilot and could no doubt get out of trouble. He could put the slow-flying gyro down almost anywhere with a fair degree of safety, although it would mean having to leave it where it landed to rust away through the ages. But to the passenger the flight must have been a nightmare.

As the gyro approached the waterfall farther up the gorge, however, the watchers felt their own hearts quicken. It was impossible to judge from where they stood whether the plane had sufficient height to clear. It certainly looked close. If Kell failed to clear the fall he would crash into it, and both he and his passenger would assuredly be killed. The gorge so narrowed there that if he made the attempt and then found the plane would not clear the fall, there was not a ghost of a chance of his turning and flying the plane to an emergency landing on flat ground near the camp.

It certainly looked as though Kell was making the attempt. The machine got closer and closer to the falls. The black walls of the gorge seemed to close in, waiting for the frail aircraft to smash itself on their crags. The young men watched with bated breath. It seemed impossible for Kell to avoid disaster. The machine appeared to be flying straight into the falls. Then at the moment when it seemed certain to disappear in a flurry of white water—well, it just didn't. The angle of observation deceived the watchers. The machine slowly rose beyond the falls. Then its landing wheels hovered with clear space between them and the smooth sweep of plunging water. They could see then that it had cleared with about twelve feet to spare. The gyro disappeared from view beyond the rim of the falls.

"Phew!" sighed Garry. "Am I relieved! Kell certainly has judgment."

"Or luck?" suggested Colin.

"You don't like passing the devil his due when he earns it, do you, Colin?" said Garry.

"Well, it's time to get moving again," Larry announced. He signed to the porters to start breaking camp. "Tex and Ted and the head guy will look after those fellers," he said. "We'll push on and see what's cooking."

"We'll come with you," Colin suggested. "Then we'll have to shove off or we'll be benighted. If we climb up beside the fall and strike over the ridge from there we should easily catch up with our party before dark."

"O.K. Let's go."

It took about an hour to do the two miles from the old camp up the 200-foot clamber by the waterfall and across the surprisingly broad alp to where the gyro had landed. As the three young men tramped across the turf, Kinchinga soared before them in all its glory. From that green valley it looked even more impressive than it did from the snow-capped ridge.

"Well, well, well," shouted Green as he spotted the others approaching. "The reception committee's a bit late, isn't it?"

"Glad to see you again, Green," said Garry, shaking his hand. "Congratulations on getting here alive."

Kell appeared from the other side of the plane.

"Congratulations, Kell, on a fine bit of flying," Garry tendered.

"Still snooping, eh?" rasped Kell. "You just about win the belt for snooping."

"Cut it out, Kell," urged Larry. "McGowan and Meighan just dropped over to see how things were going."

"Well, now they know," snapped Kell.

"I'll bet you're the sort of fellow, Kell," Colin said, "who would put up a 'Beware of the Dog' notice, even if you didn't have a dog, for fear someone might drop in."

"You've got the deuce of a manner with you, Kell," said Green. "It's no wonder you can't handle the natives. You ought to read a dictionary sometime and find out what tact means. Tact is a useful little thing to have in your pocket. It's saved my life several times when I've found myself in odd spots in odd places about this odd world."

"Keep out of this," said Kell. "I say what I think, and I'm beholden to nobody."

"Well, it's your funeral. But take a word of advice. Don't think natives are animals. They're not. They're human beings. And anyway, even animals have feelings and a right to enjoy the world."

"Cut out the preaching," implored Kell.

"Come along, Garry," suggested Colin. "Apparently this valley isn't big enough to hold us all. Cheerio, Green. So long, Larry."

"Good luck, pal," said Garry, shaking Larry Elmer's hand. "May the best man stand on Kinchinga's top first."

Garry and Colin struck up the ridge and arrived at their own camping-place with an hour to dark. They assisted in the settling-down for the night.

The following day Sir Peter's party turned a bend in the valley and Kinchinga was revealed to most of the members for the first time. The valley dissolved into the steep, broken ice terrain of a glacier in the next seven miles, so Sir Peter decided it was time to make for the ridge. The long string of porters struggled up an oblique path pioneered by the Europeans, and after many hours came to the snow of the ridge. Once above the snow-line most of the Europeans would be there for practically all of the rest of the journey. A camp was established that night in the shelter of a rocky promontory on the ridge. Garry was amazed that he could sleep so comfortably in the snow. The tent was wind-proof. He was well wrapped up in an eider-lined sleeping-bag on an

air-filled mattress, which kept his body from contact
with the cold of the snow.

Another two days brought the party to the foot of the
main bulk of Kinchinga. They had walked over a snow
saddle and come to rock which they could almost literally
touch and say was Kinchinga at last.

Here, on scree in the shelter of a rock gulley, the
Kalmet men laid down their burdens. This would be
the base camp. Here, Sir Peter decided, they would
make a cache of their stores and the Kalmet men were
dismissed. The porters, after being paid off, filed away
along the ridge. They had done their job of bringing
the main stores to the base camp, and were now discarded
as the exhausted charge-chamber of a rocket would be
discarded. They did not mind that. They had little
love for snow and ice, and they had been well rewarded
by their standards for the work they had done.

The only natives remaining were the six Sherpas,
skilled mountain men who would carry the equipment
still needed and who could, within a few days, return
from the higher camps and bring up any further stores
that might be required.

Then the real ascent of Kinchinga began at last. On
the first day, starting at 3 a.m. with a full moon, the
party climbed 3000 feet to establish Camp I at approximately 17,500 feet. The summit lay 6000 feet above
them. But the last 6000 feet was the real climb, and it
might take weeks to cover that ground. Now the climbers
wore light wind-proof clothes and wool-lined helmets.
All the clothing was close-fitting at wrists, ankles, and
necks to keep out the cold. The wind was bitter and
the sun was torture. Only in this fantastic world could
a man risk sunstroke and frostbite simultaneously. All
members wore dark goggles to shut out the blinding
glare of sun on a world of pure white. For snow-blindness
was not the least danger.

Garry had strapped the small radio receiver and
transmitter to his back. His transmitter was the only
means of getting his story out to the world. That night

in Camp I he listened to the report of the American party's progress.

The three lads and Kell had also reached the base of the mountain and had begun climbing. Green had apparently been left at the base camp. That did not surprise Garry in view of Green's vehemently expressed dislike of high places. Kell was apparently accompanying the lads as far as practicable, taking his radio with him. As the Mercer Press was sponsoring the expedition, it was only natural that they wanted full details of progress.

Kell was not a mountaineer, so it was doubtful if he would get very far, but he would obviously choose as his own more or less permanent camp a vantage-point whence he could observe the progress of the three youths.

Early the following day Sir Peter and Colin climbed the 400-foot rock wall above Camp I to survey the next section of the route. It was a stiffish bit of rock-climbing, and Sir Peter was quite content to let the brilliant younger man lead. There is no cairned path up a remote Himalayan giant. Sometimes what seems from a distance a negotiable route is at close quarters a chaotic tumble of rocks and glacier ice completely obliterating all view of recognizable landmarks. It would, naturally, be foolish to attempt to progress haphazardly and hope for the best. A haphazardly followed route might end in sheer cliffs, and the best climber in the world is beaten unless he can find foot- and hand-holds.

Some plan of campaign has to be arrived at, but as closer acquaintance with the mountain reveals new features, the plan has to be amended accordingly. At a distance what might appear a well-bound ridge might, when skirted and viewed from a different angle, reveal an unclimbable cleft. If that ridge had been decided upon as a possible route then another way would have to be sought, always bearing in mind that whatever way was chosen would have to show a continuous trail to the mountain-top.

It could be likened to one of those old-fashioned maze puzzles, and indeed Garry had done so for the enlightenment of his readers. " The only difference between a maze puzzle and a mountain," he wrote, " is that a maze puzzle has only one route from its outside to the goal in the middle. A mountain usually has several possible routes, but the principle is the same. In the maze you follow a lane and then find it comes to a dead end, or, as the mountaineer says, it ' won't go.' So you retrace your steps and try another way. That is the way a mountaineer finds his way ; but he does not often have to retrace his steps, because he surveys the mountain from a distance and from different angles, and by observation decides which route will most likely take him to the summit, and then follows it."

That was why Colin and Sir Peter climbed the Garden Wall, as they had christened the precipice. From the top of its narrow ridge they could see Kinchinga once more. Below them were the tents of Camp I. Sir Peter decided that the best way to Camp II would be to skirt the wall for half a mile, then climb a diagonal well-broken ledge which appeared to lead to steep snow. It was probably a long trudge in snow to a farther rocky excrescence which was at a height, Sir Peter estimated, of about 20,000 feet. But in the clear atmosphere of such tremendous heights and in such a gigantic landscape it was a sadly difficult task to judge distances. What might look like a five minutes' stroll would probably prove to be two hours' hard toiling.

Sir Peter and Colin descended to the camp. Colin found that he was feeling far from well when he got there. In that rarefied atmosphere he had climbed too vigorously, and now he was attacked by mountain sickness. Sir Peter decided to stay at Camp I for the day. It would give all six white men a chance to get acclimatized before climbing into a still rarer atmosphere. Meanwhile the six Sherpas, under the efficient guidance of Kipar, had returned to the Base Camp. The six white men spent the day looking at the mountains, dozing, or talking. Even Graham, the botanist, became talkative, and delivered a long lecture on saxifrages which, be it said to their everlasting shame, lulled the other members most pleasantly to sleep.

Late in the afternoon the Sherpas returned laden with more equipment for reinforcing Camp I. Therein lay the reason for establishing a number of camps. Food and equipment must be taken high enough on the mountain to provide a jumping-off place for the culminating attempt on the summit. The porters could transport equipment from camp to camp, travelling back and forth between them over a route defined by the white men.

The following day Sir Peter and Colin set off to establish Camp II. As they had anticipated, the route "went," and four hours of climbing brought them to the shadow of the rocky outcrop. They pitched tents and dropped the 60 pounds or so of equipment that they had brought with them, and returned to Camp I. The next day the whole party, fully laden, followed the two pioneers to the selected site. They had all become pretty well acclimatized by now, and as there was no particular technical ability required they were well established by midday. After lunch the Sherpas returned for further loads, and this time Graham and Read went forward to reconnoitre Camp III.

The two scientists found that once round the rocky outcrop they encountered a snow arête—a ridge of hard-packed snow a thousand feet long, sloping steeply to the south and disappearing below the clouds which formed a fleecy bed 2000 feet below. To the north the arête fell away sheer for 1500 feet—a horrifying drop. The arête appeared to be solid snow, with no rock foundation. When the two men reached it the sun was shining strongly and they prudently decided not to risk crossing. The sun will soften snow, and if the weight of a man is applied to it large slabs will often peel off, avalanching down the steep slope at an ever-increasing speed and carrying the unfortunate climber to destruction. Obviously the arête was the only possible route to the final ridge of Kinchinga, at any rate from this position

It would have to be traversed early in the morning before the sun had a chance to soften the snow, which, during the bitter cold of the night, would be frozen into a safe, compact mass.

Graham and Read returned to Camp II to report. The arête was two hours' climb from the camp, so réveillé was very early the next morning. Read was not feeling bright when he wakened. He was suffering from a bout of mountain sickness. Dr. Dodd advised him to stay at the camp, and volunteered to stay with him.

The remaining ten men arrived at the arête before dawn. Four of the Sherpas returned at once to Camp II to pick up further equipment. By the time they returned the other six men had crossed the 1500 feet of the arête, and the two Sherpas had returned and were waiting on the civilization side. One of them was Kipar. He was an experienced and safe mountain man. He roped up his fellows and ventured on to the arête, testing it as he went with an ice-axe. It was still firm, and seemed likely to stay so for some time. The new loads were dumped on the Kinchinga side and Kipar escorted the other porters on the return traverse. The five other Sherpas then went back to Camp II. They would be under the direction of Doc Dodd and Read and, if necessary, would descend to the Base Camp for further supplies.

Kipar then crossed the arête for the fifth time that day. Garry and Colin had by this time deposited their first loads and had returned to the arête. The three men shouldered the new loads and set off after Sir Peter and Graham, who were trying to find a suitable site for Camp III. Colin had by now learned patience. Every movement now had to be slow, rhythmic, and deliberate, owing to the tax on the lungs of the slightest exertion. A dozen steps at normal pace would produce panting, a furious beating of the heart, and the rawness in the throat that a long, hard run at sea-level would produce.

Garry was beginning to think that he could better serve the expedition by leaving his radio at Camp III and carrying only essential equipment. If he could carry 40 pounds of gear to Camp IV it would help considerably in the final assault.

The three men came up with Sir Peter and Graham to leeward of another snow ridge. This was not so dangerous as the arête. Its slope was easier. Nevertheless it was steep enough to necessitate the cutting of steps in the hard-frozen snow with ice-axes ; and if anyone overbalanced, he would be travelling so fast at the end of a slope nearly a mile long that he would certainly be killed. The two older men were resting. They had not so far been able to find a suitably protected camp site. The smooth round hump of the ridge a few feet higher up would be flat enough to pitch tents on, but the impracticability of that was demonstrated by the mist of blown snow streaming over their heads.

Sir Peter decided to move on. Kipar, who had been on the move all day, grinned and nodded that he was not yet whacked, and was ready for more. So the party roped up at long intervals and set out along the ice steps hacked by Sir Peter and Graham.

Then the blizzard came with startling suddenness. One moment there was clear blue sky although the sun was hidden beyond the ridge. The next moment the men were enveloped in swirling snow so dense that it almost blotted out the light. Sir Peter, who was leading, called to the others to advance slowly towards him. Gingerly they felt their way along. Where Sir Peter waited the snow slope was flattened somewhat, although it was still too severe for a man to stand without the aid of cut steps.

The crampons—the spiked metal sandals strapped to their boots—enabled the men to squat without fear of slipping. Despite the carefully designed woollen clothing and wind-proof outer garments, the cold crept in to their bodies. They huddled together in the white-swirling, shrieking gloom. For nearly two hours they crouched there, waiting for the blizzard to abate.

" Personally I'd like to be reading a nice, exciting

adventure story in a comfortable chair in front of a great cheery fire," groaned Colin.

" About something exciting—like mountaineering, eh ? " suggested Garry.

" Not for mine," said Graham. " The chair and the fire—yes. But I'd like——"

" A nice dry-as-dust treatise on botany perhaps," suggested Colin.

" Certainly not," Graham protested. " I'm quite partial to a good thriller—and the more bodies the better."

" We're forgetting Kipar," Sir Peter said. " Kipar, you think we white men very mad, no ? "

" All ri'," answered Kipar with a throaty chuckle. " Me get money. You no get money. You mad. Me all ri'."

The others laughed.

" Where you like be most now ? " asked Graham.

Kipar did not understand.

" You, Kipar," Graham persisted. " You no like mountains. You like wife, babies ? You like be home ? You like eat big eat ? Make tummy fat ? "

" Me all ri'," answered Kipar with an indifferent suggestion that he did not care much where he was.

The party relapsed into silence. It is very difficult to feel happy when you are four miles high on a mountain, weeks of weary walking from the nearest, most primitive civilization, and enveloped by a seemingly eternal, bitter cold gloom.

After two hours the blizzard still showed no signs of abating.

" We've got to do something about this," announced Sir Peter at last. " We can't sit here indefinitely. Equally certainly we can't move away, because we can't see where we're going. And you'd find you had an awful long way to go if you stepped on to a snow bridge that Nature didn't design to take the weight of a man. It looks to me as if we're already at Camp III."

" You don't mean camp here on an exposed snow

slope that's nearly as steep as a wall ? " protested Garry. " If you rolled over in bed you'd roll three miles."

" You'd roll two miles and fall half a mile," corrected Sir Peter. " Personally I'd risk anything rather than freeze to death—a most unpleasant way of passing out. A two-mile roll in the snow would at least be exhilarating."

" But we can't erect the tents here," said Colin.

" You'll note," said Sir Peter, " that the slope just here is less severe than in other parts of the ridge. We shall cut out a platform. We shall start doing that now. We can't work too strenuously in this atmosphere for too long at a stretch, so I suggest we do three or four minutes a shift. We can break up the hard snow with the ice-axes and kick the loose stuff down the slope. We can cut a cosy, flat little niche without a great deal of trouble."

Garry took his ice-axe and began hacking away at the snow. The others took over in turn. After about two hours they had cut out a flat ledge about twelve feet by six feet. The surrounding snow wall made a welcome protection from the wind. The tents were erected by frozen, fumbling hands, and air mattresses inflated with difficulty. Once inside the shelters and insulated from the snow by a cushion of air, the five men began to thaw out. As the cold went out, cheerfulness came in. Portable stoves were soon boiling strong coffee and dehydrated meat stew.

Then came the question of the disposition of the climbers in the tents. It was easy to arrange that Sir Peter and Graham should occupy one tent. They were both scholars and addicted to philosophy, so they could entertain each other—and that was an important point. No one knew how long the blizzard might last. That meant they would have to lie there in the tiny tents with nothing to do and only their thoughts and their voices to kill the appalling monotony. After a day or two in such constant intimate company, men whose temperaments were badly matched could come to entertain almost murderous thoughts towards each other.

Garry and Colin were also well matched. They had youth and a devotion to sport in common. The odd man out was Kipar. He had to go in one tent or the other. He was a cheerful and likeable fellow, but neither camp wanted him. The sole reason was that the Sherpas had a pronounced objection to bathing or changing their clothes too frequently. In the open air of a mountain-side that did not matter. But to be cooped up with such a person in the confines of a tent measuring six feet square with a bare three feet six inches of head-room was a different kettle of fish. Indeed, a kettle of fish—even very stale ones—would have been preferable.

The argument was conducted in lofty language lest Kipar should understand what it was all about. None of them wanted to hurt his feelings.

"The odoriferous condition of our most estimable confrère presents a problem of considerable magnitude," said Sir Peter. "You two, being younger men and therefore more easily adaptable, should offer ungrudging hospitality to his—er—highness." Sir Peter laid meaningful stress on the last word.

That was typical of the language in which the argument was conducted. Garry and Colin protested vigorously and rhetorically. In the end the argument ended, as do so many arguments, with a common consent to abide by the dictates of Fate as intimated by the tossing of a coin.

By incredible chance Garry was able to produce a penny. It was tossed with a minimum of exuberance lest it disappear for ever in the awful chasms of the Himalayas. The result was that Garry and Colin won Kipar.

Kipar grinned broadly. His comment dumbfounded them. "Plenty palaver all 'cause me smell."

Garry and Colin found that their senses became quickly accustomed to an inescapable sensation, and after a few hours Kipar's unhygienic state was scarcely noticeable.

Garry managed to get the radio going and got news of

the rival party's progress. Apparently Kell had posted himself in a camp on Barren Kot, a knob 500 feet above the level of the lower ridge. It commanded a view along the sharp edge all the way to the summit. From there Kell could see with powerful binoculars the progress of the youngsters. The three lads had established two further camps, and then they too had been halted by the blizzard. Kell's estimate gave their height as 22,500 feet. Sir Peter's barometer gave his Camp III position as 22,000 feet. That meant that the Americans were in a better position. But then, Kell's estimate could not be accurate.

Garry and Colin had felt such exhaustion and fatigue during the climbing that their feelings had been to let the race go hang. Quite relaxed and lying on their backs in the tent, their bodies no longer aching dreadfully with the torture of movement, they experienced again the great urge to be on the move, to achieve the summit of Kinchinga. Garry was even beginning to hope he might reach the summit himself, although he was in fact merely supernumerary to the expedition.

The blizzard lasted for thirty-eight hours. That meant two nights in the tents. On the second morning the sky was clear blue again. The tents were almost completely buried in snow.

Garry and Colin emerged in high spirits. Kipar's cheerfulness and comical remarks had enlivened their forced imprisonment. Sir Peter and Graham, on the other hand, were both in foul tempers and snapping angrily at every remark or action the other made. Colin and Garry exchanged grins and winked.

"Don't know what you fellows find so darned pleasing!" grunted Sir Peter.

"Kipar kept us amused," explained Colin. "You ought to try him some time. He's a good tonic for sluggish liver."

"You can keep him," snapped Sir Peter, his face puckering into an expression of wry distaste.

Camp III seemed to have settled very snugly into the

8

landscape, so Kipar returned to Camp II for further supplies. These he and the other Sherpas brought up during the next two days.

In the meantime the four white men pushed ahead to find a site for what they hoped would be the last real camp before the attack on the summit—Camp IV.

The work of the Sherpas was practically complete. They delivered about 300 pounds weight of supplies at Camp III and then returned to Camp II. There Read and the Doc, having checked the items that had been transported to the higher camps, gave the porters instructions to return to the Base Camp and wait, thus conserving the precious food so laboriously carried high up on the mountain.

CHAPTER VII

MAROONED

ONCE on the move the strain began to make itself felt again. Limbs seemed leaden and reluctant to obey the wishes of the brain. In fact, their brains also seemed to go numb. Thoughts involved too much mental activity, so the four men plodded on mechanically in a sort of mental black-out. The depression was so appalling that Garry wondered that one or all of them did not crack and about turn and stumble all the way back, down those frightening snow slopes and precipitous rocks, down the tortuous gorges, across India to a boat and the sea and home and comfortable arm-chairs and fires and noisy, crowded streets. The desire to do so was so insistent that it was a form of torture. But Garry clenched his teeth, and made up his mind that he would not be the first to give in. Maybe the fact that each of them made up his mind that he would not be the first to crack was the reason that none of them did.

The race now meant nothing. No power on earth

could spur either Colin or Garry to further effort. There remained only a slow, dogged determination not to crack. Every now and again the men halted and rested, breathing loudly, gasping for precious air. Sir Peter's watch showed the time. There was fifteen minutes only allowed for each halt. As the fifteen minutes showed up, they all went through the agony of taking up their loads and pushing on again. To extend the fifteen minutes by fifteen seconds would be risking surrender to their weakness. Once the rests were extended, the men might lose inclination to move farther. And it was by common consent that the four had set out determined that Camp IV should be the final camp before the great assault. Only one halt of more than fifteen minutes was allowed—that was one full, infinitely precious hour for lunch.

At five o'clock the snow ridge ended in rock. They could go no farther via the slope on the sheltered side of the ridge. The rock was not steep on the ridge, but to east and west—or so it seemed from what they could see beyond the ridge—it fell away in sheer, smooth, impossible cliffs. Sir Peter, leading, cut steps up the last steep snow slope. The air was perfectly still and crisply cold. But above the ridge the wind shrieked in icy fury. As Sir Peter's head rose above the level of the ridge and caught the blast he was almost blown off his balance. He leaned inwards to the slope, and on hands and knees crawled on to the flat top of the ridge. To stand would have meant being blown right off the mountain. The others followed him one by one. A crawl of about twenty yards in that flailing, shrieking snow and ice brought them to the shelter of a small rock outcrop.

Sir Peter's watch came out and the time was noted. Each hoped that here camp would be established, but each knew also that there was still an hour of good light, and that the tumble of rock above them was not technically difficult. It was also obvious that the rock could be climbed while keeping on the lee side of the ridge without getting too close to the exposed cliffs to the east. The watch-hand covered the dial markings which indicated fifteen minutes long before the breathing of the men had returned to normal.

Then began the exhausting climb of 400 feet to the top of the rock. Each foot-hold had to be carefully found ; pain-racked fingers scrabbled for holds, found them ; aching arms hauled heavy, panting bodies upwards—ever upwards.

And so the 400-foot climb was accomplished. By great good fortune there was a sort of roofless cave near the top—a snow-floored declivity with walls on three sides. None of the men recollected ever having experienced such luxury, for here was the perfect shelter. Tents were erected and mattresses inflated, while Graham fussed around with a primus and produced such appetizing food smells that all of them were slobbering saliva long before the food reached their mouths. Luxuriously relaxed, and feeling the warmth of hot food and coffee seeping through their bodies, the four men eagerly discussed the final phase of the expedition. Night was descending fast, and any further reconnaissance was out of the question. The morrow would show how near or far they were from victory.

The weather was the main consideration now. So far the climb had been pursued mainly on the lee side of one of the three main ridges. The Americans had been climbing on the lee of the central ridge. Now the ridge the Englishmen had followed joined with the breathtaking black rock cliffs to the east. These cliffs dropped sheer almost from the summit. Even if the climbers ventured on them, they could not do a rock-climbing job of even a hundred feet at that altitude and in such perishing cold. And the cliffs extended upwards for at least another twelve hundred feet.

The only possible route was along the final snow ridge, almost razor sharp, and falling almost sheer away on either side. Obviously weather conditions would have to be perfect. Although the day's climb had been strenuous because of the altitude, it had also been accomplished in calm weather. Yet the last few hundred feet had shown

THEN BEGAN THE EXHAUSTING CLIMB OF 400 FEET
TO THE TOP OF THE ROCK.

that across the crest of the ridge, despite the calm on the lee, a tremendous storm was blowing. Any creature venturing on the last section in such a gale would be swept away in an instant.

" So," said Garry, " we sit and twiddle our thumbs and wait for the weather to break itself down ? "

" Yes," replied Sir Peter, in a manner that suggested he was perfectly content to sit patiently sipping coffee till kingdom come.

" And how long do you suppose we will have to sit here ? " Garry asked.

" That's impossible to answer."

" Maybe it won't break at all," Colin suggested.

" In that case," answered Sir Peter, " we sit here until we reach the safe limit of our food and heating resources."

" And then go down—with no mountain-top in the bag ? " asked Garry.

" Precisely."

" After all this effort ! That would just about break my heart," groaned Garry sombrely. " Wouldn't it just make you feel like kicking all the dogs in Christendom out of spite ! "

" Why should it ? " demanded Sir Peter, still in his calm, matter-of-fact mood. " We strive with every power we've got to win. If we don't win, we say : ' Better luck next time.' We go—but we shall come back."

" Without me," said Garry. " I'll try anything once. There'll be no twice with me so far as Himalayan giants are concerned. And talking of giants—we haven't met the famous Kinchinga horror yet."

" We're not to the top yet," Sir Peter reminded him.

" You don't mean you really believe . . ." Garry ventured. " You surely didn't expect to see it ? "

" No, of course not. Only . . ."

" Only there might have been something in the story," Colin chimed in.

" Most fantastic stories have some slight basis of truth," Garry said.

" Well, this one is all arrant nonsense," asserted Sir Peter.

For a while all four men were silent and thoughtful. The only sounds were the noisy consumption of hot soup and the faint whine of the storm beyond the sheltered declivity. Garry experienced that delicious snug sensation of being tucked up and warm and comfortable while outside all the contending blasts of heaven shrieked their anger and fury at their inability to invade the sanctuary of those tiny tents set securely near the summit of a forbidding giant nearly five miles high above the sea. He could not help but shudder at the thought that many weeks of bitter cold, and desolation of snow and ice, and torture of lungs and limbs must ensue before he could again enjoy normal climate and civilization.

" I'll confine my mountaineering in future to a Sunday afternoon walk up Highgate Hill," he vowed.

A little desultory conversation followed.

" To-morrow," announced Sir Peter, addressing Colin and Garry, " you two will return to Camp III and bring up a further load of supplies. Kipar and the other porters will have brought up a further load of stuff by now."

" Will we bring Kipar up here to Camp IV ? " asked Colin.

" The fewer men here the better," said Sir Peter. " He had better lodge at Camp II with Read and Dodd."

" I wonder how those two are getting along ? " pondered Graham.

" They'll be all right and quite safe at Camp II."

" A bit rough on them," sympathized Garry.

" In a way I suppose it is," agreed Sir Peter. " But they are serving a very useful purpose. They are supervising the transport of supplies to the higher camps. That's a pretty responsible job. The Sherpas haven't the necessary mental equipment for deciding what we shall want and how and when we shall want it. Read and Dodd are ideally situated for such a job at the half-way camp."

The four men, physically fatigued and weary, now began to feel the weight of sleepiness, and almost immediately sorted themselves into their respective tents and turned in.

As Garry drifted into sleep he began thinking of the great race. In such comparative, and therefore delicious, comfort it was pleasant to dwell on the exciting prospects of the race, although he knew that when the strain of movement came again on the morrow he would wish the race to perdition. Thinking that the greatest pleasure would come when it was all over and he could think back on his experiences, his mind clouded over with sleep.

The following morning he woke stiff and cold and miserable. He woke Colin, and then went to the other tent to wake Sir Peter and Graham. Graham prepared breakfast, after the consumption of which Garry felt much better. Then he and Colin took food in rucksacks and set off on the journey back to Camp III. When they reached the base of the 400-foot rock climb they ventured to the top of the ridge. The terrific gale still blew with unabated intensity, the blown snow streaming over their heads like an endless procession of white, wailing ghosts. Once on the top they wormed along on their bellies until they could see the other ridge, now about four miles distant—a bastion to the main peak. Garry got his binoculars and scoured the ridge. At last he found what he sought.

The atmosphere and the immensity of the mountain suggested that the other ridge was little more than a stone's throw away instead of four miles. That was why it was hard to believe that the two tiny dark spots on a snow slope were actually the tents of the Americans. As Garry watched he saw black dots moving about them and pointed them out to Colin.

" What chances have they got ? " Garry asked.

Colin screwed up his eyes and puckered his lips, and

Garry heard the voice of mountain experience reply : " The same chance as us. They've got to wait for the weather too."

" And then ? "

" It's an even chance. The party that can find a route first and stick it out will win."

Garry and Colin wormed their way back to the lee of the ridge and began the descent to Camp III. They arrived there about three hours after the halt for lunch, and found the fresh loads brought up by the porters, who had since returned to the lower levels of the mountain. Colin examined the stuff they found in the tents.

" We've got enough now to stay here on the mountain for nearly four weeks," he announced. " We can get a fair amount of this up when we return to Camp IV, and if we want any more we can come back for it. I hope the weather will give us a break and save that bother."

Garry switched on his radio, which he had left at that camp, and transmitted the latest news of the party's progress to his base station near Darjeeling, whence it would be conveyed to the *Gazette*. On the receiver he heard the news that Kell was putting out for the Mercer Press. It was a highly coloured narrative about " these three intrepid American lads standing on the springboard ready for the final attack on one of the world's mightiest unconquered mountains. Battling against blizzard and physical torment almost beyond imagination, with teeth gritted tightly, they have dared the dangers of Kinchinga with unparalleled determination and heroism. . . ."

Garry switched the radio off with a disgustedly muttered : " Hokum ! "

The following morning the two young men loaded themselves with fresh packs and set out on the laborious return to Camp IV. There was very little cloud. The sun rose clearly, and even in that low temperature its rays soon caused the climbers acute discomfort. It made the ascent even more trying than on the previous occasion. About two o'clock it slid down the other side of the ridge to the west and both men were thankful indeed to see it go.

As they got higher they noticed that the wind-swept stream of snow had considerably diminished.

" The storm's blowing itself out," gasped Colin, the sudden excitement of realizing that the mountain might soon be theirs causing his heart to race and thus making his breathing more laboured still.

But Garry already felt too much strain on heart and limb to put one more ounce of exertion into his efforts. He could see that Colin, despite the strain and the heavy mental inertia that was so difficult to combat, was urging upward with impatient excitement. When they reached the rocks once more and climbed on to the crest of the ridge the wind was little more than a strong breeze. They could stand in comfort, and were in no danger at all of being blown off the mountain. Colin, with every show of impatience, grunted his way to a place that would provide a view of the Americans' camp. He was anxious to observe what move they might be making. He extended his hand eagerly for Garry's binoculars and trained them towards where they had previously seen the tents. Then he pushed the binoculars quickly into Garry's hands.

" Look," he tried to shout, but his voice cracked into a heavy, wheezing sound. " They're mad. They'll kill themselves."

Garry saw three minute specks roped together that seemed to move with the slowness of the hand of a clock advancing up the white ridge. They were silhouetted against the deep blue sky. The Americans had started their assault. Garry looked at Colin almost expecting him to go bounding like a chamois up the 400-foot cliffs and straight to the summit. But Colin's mouth was set in a grim line and his eyes were fixed on the distant ridge. He put out his hand for the binoculars again.

"That's inexperience," he announced. "They'll kill themselves."

"But the storm has passed, hasn't it?" Garry asked.

"That isn't the danger. It's their inexperience. Those kids have done marvels, but all the same they should never have been allowed to attempt the climb."

"Jealous?" suggested Garry.

"Of course I am," retorted Colin. "I'm human. And I want to bag Kinchinga myself. But I'm hanged if I'd take a risk like that to do it."

"I'm a greenhorn myself when it comes to mountains," Garry reminded him. "And I'm bust if I can see any risk in their having a crack at it while the going's good."

"They've been waiting for the storm to die away," Colin explained. "They've been waiting nearly all day. And all day the sun has been shining on that snow. The sun softens it up. It looks all right, but it's soggy, and under a climber's weight it might peel off and take him with it to kingdom come. That cornice they're approaching right now must be in a treacherous condition. It should never be attempted except in the morning before sun-up."

"Can't we shout?" asked Garry.

"Of course we can shout, but they'd never hear us."

Garry looked at the cornice that Colin had indicated. It was near where the ridge merged into the last 2000-foot rocky hump of the mountain. There would be a slope of snow on the other side, but Colin and Garry could see by the shadows cast by the westering sun that on the east the snow was sheer and the face slightly concave, something like an immense white wave rearing and on the point of breaking.

The binoculars passed frequently between Colin and Garry, who could not leave the spot, so fearful were they for the safety of the Americans. Their hearts beat faster as the lads neared the fearful cornice. They felt so utterly impotent, incapable of doing anything but crouch and watch.

At last the three figures reached the cornice. They merged into one solid dark spot. Obviously a conference was in progress. Then a figure detached itself and moved on to the cornice. Both Garry and Colin audibly sighed relief when the figure reached the dark mass of rock and could no longer be seen. The leader had successfully completed the traverse. The second man followed. He, too, got safely across. The third started. He was just a little more than half-way across when he seemed to slide slowly downwards.

Garry had the binoculars. " He's gone," he shouted " It's crumbling."

The figure moved with increasing speed and finally stopped abruptly, swaying to and fro. The rope held him. Meantime the snow that he had displaced went pouring into the chasm, taking more and more snow with it until it became an awe-inspiring avalanche—a tremendous white comet streaking into the valley. Nearly half a minute later the roar and thunder of it reached the ears of Garry and Colin.

And still the dark figure dangled against the whiteness. The Englishmen groaned. The effort of moving at that altitude was so exhausting that they could not believe that the other two lads could summon the strength to haul their comrade to safety. Yet bit by bit the tiny figure got closer to the dark mass of rock. Colin and Garry winced at the thought of performing such a physical feat in their present condition, and marvelled at the superhuman effort of the American lads.

" Well, they've got what it takes," grunted Garry.

" And good luck to them," added Colin.

As the avalanche gathered into its headlong plunge more and more snow, the effect was to undermine the cornice until at last it could stand no longer and collapsed, leaving a ragged gap about 40 feet across and 150 feet deep. The spectacle of hundreds of tons of snow crashing into the abyss was breath-taking. And above the turmoil the infinitely small figure of the American lad still dangled. Garry and Colin watched until they knew that he was safe.

Colin looked perturbed.

" They're all alive, and they can thank their lucky stars for that," he said. " But they're in a nasty hole just the same. If their route won't go they can't get back. That gap is impassable and that snow cornice must have taken years to form. They haven't a hope of bridging the gap."

" Then that means," concluded Garry, " that they've got to get to the summit and descend by way of *our* ridge ? "

Colin nodded. " It's their only chance. And looking at those rocks now with the air clear and still, I'd say their chances weren't bright. Getting to the top of any Himalayan peak is no foregone conclusion. Come along. We'd better get up and break the news to Sir Peter. We'll have to do something about it."

Garry and Colin completed the last 400 feet of ascent. They found the camp deserted. Sir Peter and Graham had left a note informing them that they were going to do a bit of reconnaissance now that the weather had piped down. It was an hour before they returned. They had seen the avalanche, but had not seen the other party at all. Garry and Colin told them the details. Sir Peter's face clouded over.

Graham cooked a meal, and while they ate it they conducted a council of war.

" Unless we can work quickly and devise a workable plan of campaign those young idiots will perish," said Sir Peter. " Obviously the camp you saw was intended to be their last camp. Above that level they would carry only sufficient equipment and food to bivouac. From their last camp to the summit and back should be only a matter of two days if they found a route. Therefore we can presume that they have very little in the way of food."

" So far as we can see," said Colin, " their only chance is to get to the summit and then come down to our ridge."

" Exactly," agreed Sir Peter. "That is, *if* they can get to the summit. And even if it's plain sailing, I doubt they'd get down to here in under four or five days. At high altitude on a mountain food is of supreme importance. Without it your vitality drops and you're almost helpless. They'll be pretty weak if they try to eke the food out. Another point is that it won't be plain sailing. Graham and I have seen enough this afternoon to convince us that Kinchinga is no easy nut to crack. We got far enough north to see that the rock face those lads will have to climb is not so easy as it looked. It was well-broken rock, but when you get round far enough to see it in profile you can see that it's almost impossibly steep. The slabs tend to lean outwards. And for our part we haven't found a likely route either. Every direction we tried the slope seemed to get steeper and steeper, and I can see no likely route up the 100-foot pitch of rock. Above that it looks like a workable snow slope to the summit."

" What is so beastly exasperating," said Graham, " is that they're only four miles away, and they're as out of touch with us as they'd be four thousand miles away."

" I wonder if they're eating as well as we are," Colin pondered. "Or I wonder if they realize the position and are rationing themselves right away."

" So the immediate problem is how to get grub to them," said Garry.

" If we try to get our grub to them it means . . ." started Colin thoughtfully.

" We'll run dangerously short ourselves," concluded Graham.

" And we'll have less time at our disposal and less chance of putting Kinchinga in the bag," Colin reflected ruefully.

" The important point now is to save the lives of those

three idiots," snapped Sir Peter, and his voice was so edged that it was an admonishment.

"Well, there's only one way I can think of for getting grub up to those kids," said Garry, "and that's by aeroplane."

"We're weeks of travelling from any aeroplane," protested Graham.

"Kell's autogyro is just above the Banghiri Gorge."

"That could fly no higher than the Gorge."

"I know. But if I got to it I could fly it down to a regular airfield, pick up a high-altitude kite, and drop food to them that way."

"It sounds all right when you say it quickly," said Sir Peter. "But even that is going to take many days. And anyway, how do you think you can drop food on to a mountain? If you dropped a parcel it would bounce once and right down into the chasms."

"I've got an idea about that," said Garry. "I think I can do it, and I'm going to have a crack at it."

"It's utterly fantastic and impossible," asserted Sir Peter.

"Well, we've got to do something, haven't we?" demanded Garry with some heat. "We can't just sit here and talk till doomsday. I'm beginning to see the whole thing now. You and Graham can try to make the summit. If you do, you might be able to go down towards the other ridge, and if there's a way up you could guide the kids towards it. They'd hear you shouting if you were above them. Colin and I will go back to Camp III. Colin can bring my radio up here to you. We will try to intercommunicate at certain definite times that we can decide later. That will enable us to co-ordinate all our plans and amend them if need be. I suggest that Colin then picks up Kipar, who may be at Camp II with Read and the Doc, and that they then try to get across to the Yanks' upper camps."

"How do you think they can do that?" demanded Sir Peter.

"Well, the two ridges and Kinchinga's southern slope

form a sort of huge basin four miles across. At the base of the basin walls the slope gets easier. It's only higher up that the walls are impossibly steep. By crossing the ridge above Camp II they should be able to descend obliquely to the more gradual slopes, work round to the other ridge, and strike up on to it."

" And how long do you think that will take? " asked Sir Peter.

" Five or six days. It won't be easy."

" Five or six days cutting steps on a steep slope practically all the way! Why, it would be killing ! "

" I guess it would be pretty grim," agreed Colin. " But I'll have a crack at it. We've got to do something, haven't we ? "

" What good can that do anyway ? " pursued Sir Peter.

" If the kids can't get through, they'll probably return to the gap in the hope of finding some way across. Well, Colin and Kipar could probably sling a rope across to them. They could get food across that way and probably rig a bridge of sorts with pitons."

" How long do you think it will take you to get to an aerodrome ? " asked Sir Peter.

" Maybe three or four days. Once I lay hands on that gyroplane it's only a few hours' flying. And I won't have to pioneer a route *down* the mountain. I'll be able to descend much more quickly than we ascended, because it is not nearly so exhausting. If the kids stay in their tents and keep warm they could last out much longer than that."

" I don't think you quite realize what you're up against," suggested Graham. " A mile on a mountain isn't a ramble from Kensington to Hyde Park Corner."

" I know," replied Garry. " Everything I have suggested is going to be pretty tough going. But those kids are in danger, and we're the only people who can do anything about it. We've got to drive ourselves to the limits of endurance to save their lives."

The party of grim-faced men sat silently in the dim lamplight.

"The moon rises at three-ten," Sir Peter announced at last.

With that, the party retired.

CHAPTER VIII

McGOWAN TAKES TO THE AIR

STILL sleep-hazy and weary from the previous day's exertions, the men were up before 3 a.m. Graham cooked breakfast, and within half an hour Garry and Colin were on their way to Camp III. They knew the route well enough by now, and the fact that steps were already cut and that no snow had since fallen enabled them to travel fairly fast. They carried only a little food and no equipment, and thus the descent was less arduous. They reached Camp III at 9 a.m. There they prepared another meal. Garry meant to transmit per radio an account of the Americans' plight and their own attempts to assist them, but he found that the batteries had run down and no spares had been brought up to Camp III. That knocked on the head any plans for intercommunication. It was now unnecessary for Colin to return to Camp IV, so the two pushed on down to Camp II, which they reached six hours later. They found that Read had quite recovered from his bout of illness, and that both he and the Doc had been chafing at the inactivity at Camp II. They had keenly desired to go on, but unselfishly decided that the fewer the men to be considered on the highest parts of the mountain the greater would be the expedition's chances of success. Kipar had gone down to the Base Camp with the other Sherpas.

Garry and Colin explained to the other two what had happened on the West Ridge. After a consultation, Read and the Doc decided that as Kipar had gone down to the

9

Base Camp they should accompany Colin to the other ridge. All three realized that a high mountain was no place for a man to play around on alone. It was all right for Colin and Garry to move alone on an already established route, but any deviation from a commonly recognized trail was highly dangerous.

While Read packed food and equipment into rucksacks, Garry, the Doc and Colin climbed to the crest of the ridge and worked out a route, after which all three returned to the camp, ate a meal, and turned in.

Again Garry rose with the moon. The packs containing food and bivouac tents were prepared. After breakfast these were shouldered. Hands were shaken and " Good lucks ! " exchanged. Garry watched the three men plod up the ridge in the brilliant silver moonlight. Then he took up his own pack and continued his descent. He arrived at the deserted Camp I soon after sunrise. There were only the two tents there. He ate another meal while preparing further plans. He wondered whether to go down to the Base Camp and pick up Kipar, or take a risk and strike across to the alp above the Banghiri Gorge alone. He would save at least half a day by taking the latter course. The weather held good, so he decided to ascend the ridge and descend on the other side, which, all the time the party had been coming up, had been swept by storm. It would be just too bad if a storm blew up when he was half-way down. Weary and mentally flat though he felt, he forced himself to plod up the ridge.

At the crest he could see the West Ridge and Kinchinga in all its majesty. He was alone in the wilderness. Somewhere up on the mountain were the other men. The other camp sites were not visible, but he could be reasonably certain of their location. Due to the foreshortening effect, Camp IV seemed to be but an hour's stroll away instead of two days' almost unendurable toil. Garry cut down obliquely towards a headland beyond which he knew the alp lay.

Fortune was on his side. The weather held. He

pushed on and reached the shelter of the bluff. He pitched his tiny bivouac tent, made coffee, and cooked an omelette of dried egg. Scarcely able to keep his eyes open, he inflated his mattress, crawled into his sleeping-bag, and slept.

When he next opened his eyes the moon was up. Resisting the strong temptation to turn over and sleep again in the cosy warmth, he rose, ate, took up his pack and pushed on. Rounding the bluff provided some difficulty. Thanks to his association with such experienced and renowned climbers, Garry had learnt enough to negotiate the difficult exposed face, dangerous though the traverse was.

Once round the bluff he could see the green alp and the silver sparkle of the stream far below him. Early in the afternoon he arrived at the place where he and Colin had visited the Americans three weeks earlier. He at last espied a tent and near it the autogyro, vanes folded back, and pushed into the shelter of a cliff face and covered by a roughly built hangar of boughs. As Garry approached the tent he shouted. Instead of one man, as he expected, two men emerged. He had surmised that Green, who admitted his dislike of heights, would return to this pleasant valley once he had set the climbers safely on the mountain, leaving them to find their own route from there. Now Kell, too, came out. Garry also noticed other tents farther down the valley. Green hastened to meet Garry and shook hands.

" Well, well, well, who would have expected to see you ? " said Green. " Has there been an accident ? "

" There has," replied Garry.

Green's welcoming smile faded.

" I'm sorry to hear it," he said. " Has anyone been . . . ? "

" No ; no one's been killed," Garry reassured him. He could see from Green's obvious anxiety for details that he knew nothing of the happening of three days before. " It is not our party. It's yours."

They had by now approached close to Kell.

" Well, if it isn't our knight-errant of the news-presses ! " said Kell. " You do get around, don't you ? "

" What are you doing here, Kell ? " Garry asked.

" And what the devil has that got to do with you ? "

" Cut out the snapping. We've both got a job to do. Unless for some reason best known to yourself you've been holding out on Green and already know it, I'll tell you something that will smear that nasty grin of yours. Your three lads have made the mistake that their inexperience was sure to lead them into."

Even Kell's dark face whitened a little.

" What I want to know is why are you down here just when those young idiots chose to attack the summit."

" Are they hurt ? " asked Kell.

" I don't know. One may be. But they're all lucky to be alive. They were saved by a matter of seconds. Now they're marooned near the summit, and I've come to do something about it."

Garry gave a detailed account of the incident.

" I don't know why you left your vantage-point at such a time, Kell," he went on.

" My radio batteries went dead. I came down to get an accumulator out of the gyro," Kell replied.

" Surely you didn't come down alone ? "

" Some of the porters came with me." Kell indicated the tents farther down the valley. Garry noticed that he was carrying a revolver in a holster, and he could tell by his expression when he looked towards the tents that Kell was afraid of the natives. They had probably grown truculent again under his bullying.

" Well, I'm sorry, Kell," Garry said, " but your radio will have to wait."

" What do you mean ? "

" We've got to get those kids out of the nasty fix they're in. I've made my plans. Our party on the mountain has broken into two groups, who are taking what strategical action they can. In the meantime we've got to get food up to the kids—and quickly. That's why I want that gyroplane."

" You want it ? " repeated Kell. " But it's my gyro, and I'm plumb sure you won't get it."

" If it was a matter of your flying down and getting help it would be O.K.," Garry explained. " But it isn't as simple as that. It's practically impossible to find anyone on a mountain from a plane. It's several degrees worse than looking for a needle in a haystack. I've been on the mountain. I know its topography, and I know just where the kids are likely to be. I intend to get a high-ceiling plane and drop supplies near where we saw them last."

" You don't get the gyro," Kell repeated.

Garry was thunderstruck. " Don't you realize they're in peril of their lives ? " he demanded.

" Your scheme is utterly fantastic, and is probably a ruse to get in first with the story of the mishap."

" It's queer," said Garry, " but I only just realize I've been so worried and hustled on this rescue job that the thought of getting a story to the *Gazette* clean slipped my mind."

" My intention," said Kell, " is to keep faith with my public. I intend to take a battery from the gyro, return to the Little Tower on Barren Kot, and report the event to the world."

" Are you mad ? " expostulated Garry. " Haven't you any sense of responsibility ? "

" Certainly I have. But what can I do in the matter ? Your own party is taking some steps towards a rescue. But as for your own scheme, it is so idiotically impossible that I am perfectly justified in refusing you the plane."

" It's a chance. And it's a chance I'm going to take. It was your crazy idea that got the kids into trouble. Well, it's my crazy idea that's going to get them out."

" You don't take that gyro."

" Look here," protested Green, " you can't play at reporters when human lives are at stake."

" Keep out of this, Green," snapped Kell.

" I'm taking that machine here and now," announced Garry, and turned and walked towards the plane.

" McGowan ! " called Kell.

Garry turned. Kell held the revolver in his hand.

" McGowan, take up your pack and get back the way you came. I'm not risking having you hanging round here."

" Cut out the big bad man stuff," said Garry. " You wouldn't dare shoot."

" I'll give you just one minute to start walking. Accidents happen on mountains, and who is there to tell ? " scoffed Kell.

" There's me," snapped Green.

In a second the revolver was flying through the air and Kell was on his back on the grass.

" Thanks, Green," said Garry.

" He would have shot you all right," said Green, recovering the weapon and pocketing it. " And me too. The mountain has given him the jumps. He's just crazy with nerves. The natives keep on jabbering about the monster being on the other side of the Little Tower. I don't know whether he's scared of the mythical monster or the natives. I warned him, but he still knocks them around, and they don't like it. He knows it, and he's so darn scared he jumps at his own shadow."

Kell got to his feet, his eyes flashing with madness, his lower lip trembling, and a babble of nonsense coming from his lips. He rushed furiously at Garry, his arms flailing. Garry's fist came up like a jack-in-the-box and Kell crumpled to the ground, where he lay moaning softly.

Green assisted Garry to wheel the gyro to an open space. Kell rose, but kept his distance, fuming with frustration.

" You're sacked, Green," he ranted. " You'll pay for this. You won't get away with it."

Garry and Green ignored him. They unfolded the vanes and pinned them, checked petrol and oil.

" There's enough to get me down on to the plain, anyway," said Garry.

Green produced a map.

" There's an airfield—an R.A.F. station—at Milna," he informed Garry and pointed it out on the map.

" That's about ninety miles away," commented Garry. " I should get there in about an hour—if I can get this thing off the ground."

He started the engine. The gyroplane was a simple craft to fly. He had handled one once before, and had a fair idea of its mechanical details and behaviour in the air. The engine thermometer at last showed that the engine was operating at the right heat. Garry climbed into the cockpit and taxied across the grass to get a run. He turned the nose south—towards the Banghiri Gorge, with its forbidding black walls and the waterfall which he would literally have to hurdle.

Garry did not feel by any means comfortable. He had seen the plane, piloted by Kell, come up the gorge. It was at maximum height, and it had cleared the waterfall by less than twenty feet. True, he was now without the added weight of Green ; but, even so, under normal flying and atmospheric conditions the maximum height or ceiling of the craft would not be above fifty to a hundred feet above his present level. The chances of its lifting more than a few feet in such a short run and in such rarefied atmosphere were remote. But it was now or never. The vanes began revolving. Garry gave the engine the gun. It spluttered into a steady roar, and he went bumping over the rough grass. Even the propeller seemed to be losing a lot through slip in the thin air.

The speed was too low. He got closer to the spot where the plateau dropped away and the waterfall plunged down the steep cliff. Still the craft would not lift. Garry's heart pumped violently, and perspiration studded his forehead. Only a few yards to go and still it had not become airborne. The wheels struck a rock. The machine bounced, struck earth again and rolled drunkenly. Garry saw an arc of spray as the wheels splashed into the stream. The nose tilted forward. The waterfall was beneath him. The gyro fell nose first over the brink.

Garry thought it was the end of everything as the floor of the valley rushed towards him. He fought furiously with the controls. Then suddenly, as though realizing that it was in its native element at last, the craft was flying. It was on a level keel, the motor roared smoothly, the altimeter needle was steady. Garry breathed an immense sigh and mopped his forehead. He consulted the map and the compass and went happily on his way. A little more than an hour later he touched down at Milna airfield.

The airfield was steaming hot and dusty. The scorching heat after the intense cold of the mountain only that morning made Garry feel like wilting. He was met by several of the ground staff who ran across to identify the intruder. They escorted him to the Adjutant's office.

" I'm McGowan of the London *Gazette*," Garry introduced himself.

The Adjutant shook his hand. " I'm glad to meet you, McGowan," he said. " I am Squadron-Leader Gregory. I'm only acting O.C., I'm afraid. I guess your visit has something to do with this Kinchinga stunt. I've been following your progress on the radio. And of course I used to read your articles back home in England."

Garry grinned. " Yes, my name does seem to find its way about the world. It's a much more useful passport than any official one. And you were right. This visit is to do with the Kinchinga stunt. The American kids have bought themselves a nasty spot of bother."

He recited the story and his plan.

" I notice you've got a few of the new Fury two-seat fighter-bombers here," Garry concluded. " They would be ideal for the job."

During the recital the Adjutant's forehead puckered into a deeper and deeper frown.

" I'd like to help you, McGowan," he said at last. " But, as you can imagine, we're pretty well tied up in regulations here. The Himalayas are dangerous flying country—a forced landing means a tragedy. And if a man did bale out his chances of survival would be negligible. We are forbidden to fly over that territory. If one of our pilots were to lose his life in a flight such as you suggest there would be no end of a rumpus."

" But I'm perfectly willing and eager to fly the plane myself," persisted Garry. " I used to be a test pilot before I took up sporting journalism. And I've flown scores of tests on Whirlaways, which were the predecessors of the Furies."

The Adjutant shook his head. " That is even more out of the question."

" But don't you realize that the lives of those youngsters are at stake ? "

" I do," said Gregory.

Gregory was a middle-aged man. Garry weighed him up. He judged that he would be a good flyer, quite at home with motors and kites, but horribly ill at ease and scared stiff by red tape. As he had explained, he was acting O.C.

" I do sympathize with you," Gregory went on. " But in these matters I have no power at all. Group-Captain Sherringham is the O.C. He might waive regulations. But I doubt it."

" Can I see him ? " asked Garry.

" He is on leave at the moment—touring by car over east somewhere. Heaven only knows where he is."

" But the situation is desperate," urged Garry. " Surely in an emergency such as this . . ."

" I know how you feel," said Gregory. " And I know how I feel in the matter. But the fact remains that officialdom must have its way. I don't imagine that officialdom would find any excuse for people to go endangering their lives on remote mountains. I think its attitude would be that people do such things at their own risk and that other lives must not be endangered in getting them out of trouble. Furthermore——"

"I know all that," interrupted Garry impatiently. "I detest officialdom. And this is an affair of human lives —lives like ours."

"I know," sighed Gregory. "But if I were to sanction this flight it is not only a matter of endangering my career. I would sacrifice that at any time to save a human life. But if there were a tragedy, the consequences would be serious indeed. I have a wife and family, and I must consider their welfare."

Garry was disgusted at the weakness of the man. He turned to go, but Gregory called him back.

"McGowan, I can't tell you how terribly sorry I am that I cannot give you official sanction. And I regret that I cannot tell you where you could find a suitable machine. The only course open to you apparently is to steal one."

Garry saw the humorous twist to Gregory's mouth and the suggestion of a twinkle in his eyes. His heart warmed towards him.

"You say you knew the old Whirlaways," went on Gregory. "Perhaps you'd like to have a look at one of our Furies."

"Thanks," said Garry.

Gregory took him to the flying-field and showed him one of the planes, explaining its characteristics, its controls and its instruments.

"It's a wonderful kite," said Garry enthusiastically. "To think this marvel grew out of the old Whirlaway ! . . . Look, sir, I'd like to get to the town if I could. I want to send a—a wire before going on."

"The town is two miles away," said Gregory. "I can lend you a car."

As Garry pushed the gear lever into position, Gregory

said : " You might like to get some grub while you're in town," and grinned.

An hour later Garry returned. At a garage he had picked up two old oil cans. Into them he had packed chocolate, tinned foods, and biscuits, cramming every bit of space. These tins now rattled in the back of the car. There was also about six hundred feet of thin, strong rope.

Garry parked the car at the back of the hangar where he had found it, and reported his return to Gregory.

" Look here," said Gregory, " I've been thinking maybe you'd like a flip in one of the Furies. I'd like to take you up myself."

" I'd like it a lot," said Garry.

Gregory lifted his telephone, asked for a number, and then gave some instructions. A few minutes later Garry heard a plane engine crackle into life. Gregory handed him a flying helmet, raked out a fur-lined flying overall and boots and a couple of parachutes.

" I'll show you a bit of altitude flying," said Gregory. " You'll need these togs. It's cold five or six miles up."

" You're telling me," said Garry. " I've been up that region for weeks."

Gregory and Garry then walked out on to the flying-field and climbed into a plane that stood with its engine ticking over throatily. Gregory gave it the gun. The dry earth rose in choking clouds of dust. The machine bounced across to the head of the runway, straightened up, thundered along it, and a moment later the earth began to drop away from them. Gregory put the machine through its paces. Garry noted its behaviour carefully, got the feel of its response to the controls even though he was not piloting. Then they came in to land. Gregory touched down beautifully, and taxied up to an open hangar before throwing back the perspex cover and alighting.

" Well, thanks for the buggy ride," Garry said. " It's certainly a wizard kite."

" Perhaps you'd like to join us in the mess at tea in about fifteen minutes ? " Gregory suggested, as he removed his parachute and harness and put them on a bench.

" I'd like to," said Garry. " Thanks."

With a wave of his hand Gregory departed for the administrative quarters. Garry looked around while aircraftmen wheeled the Fury into the hangar, its nose pointing outwards. Relaxing for the moment, he suddenly felt infinitely weary. For four days he had pushed himself to the limit, knowing that human lives were in danger. He had an almost irresistible desire to close his eyes and sleep. But his job was not yet finished, and with a great effort he kept his brain alert.

He suddenly noticed that the car he had used to drive into Milna was at the back of the very hangar into which the Fury was being wheeled. After a few moments a bell sounded.

" That means tea," said one of the aircraftmen. " Squadron-Leader Gregory is expecting you in the officers' mess."

" O.K.," said Garry. " I'll be along."

Then Garry suddenly realized that Gregory was actually collaborating in his plan in a most unofficial way. He could do nothing officially, but he could not have engineered things more beautifully. Timing and circumstances were perfect. In the car were two cans of food. Here was an aeroplane that might have been designed for the job already warmed up and, as Garry had noted before, with more than sufficient fuel for his projected flight. He had a kit of high-altitude clothing. And there were two parachutes—his own and Gregory's.

Garry wasted no time. He fetched the cans from the car, bound them securely with rope, and then attached a parachute to each. He opened the bomb doors of the Fury and placed the cans in position, complete with parachutes. Then he took a length of cord of moderate strength, cut it in two and tied an end of each piece to each of the parachute rip-cord rings. Next he tied the other ends to frame brackets of the machine. It now only remained for him to take the rope, which was about

six hundred feet long, tie one end to one can, coil it
carefully so that it would unwind easily, place it on a
rack, and then tie the other end to the other can. He
then contrived, with another piece of cord fastened to
the larger rope by a rolling hitch, to arrange a sort of
automatic release for the second " bomb."

His arrangements were complete. His plan was well
thought out and carefully prepared. He had adapted
the means at his disposal to achieve the ends he desired.
He realized the impossibility of trying to drop a single can
of food individually on the mountain. It would probably
bounce and fall into a chasm. Even with a parachute
he could not be sure of its landing anywhere near where
he wanted it. But now he could be reasonably sure of the
Americans getting the food. His contraption would work
thus : When he located that part of the ridge where he
was pretty well sure they would be, he would look for some
projection or headland. He would then approach it from
a carefully selected angle, and at the right moment press
the No. 1 bomb-release button. One can with its parachute would drop from the rack. As soon as its weight
jerked on the string joining the rip-cord ring and the
plane the parachute would burst into bloom. The strain
would snap the cord at the same time, leaving the
parachute to float freely. The coiled rope would then
run out. As it neared the end the other piece of cord
tied to it would jerk the bomb-release and "bomb"
No. 2 would automatically drop from the rack. Again
the connecting cord would jerk the rip-cord and open the
second parachute. He would thus have two cans floating
down, joined by six hundred feet of rope. The rope
would straddle the projection he had selected, and as the
parachutes allowed the cans to subside, they would be
hooked up on the rocks, each acting as a counter-balance
to the other. It was something like the principle practised
by the spider when he sets a length of web floating in the
breeze, some part of its length eventually falling across
and adhering to some object in its orbit.

With a quick check of his work to satisfy himself no

mistake had been made, Garry climbed into the cockpit. He had not yet removed his flying clothes. He donned the helmet quickly. His own parachute was attached to one of the cans, but flying without a 'chute was a chance he had to take.

He pressed the starter switch and the warm engine coughed as the propeller blades whipped. Then it throbbed into deep thunder. Garry touched the throttle and the plane taxied on to the field. He took it as fast as he dared, for already figures were pouring out of doorways and racing towards him. He found the smooth runway and opened up. The ground flowed away swiftly beneath the wings. Soon the machine was air-borne. Garry handled the controls with deep and happy satisfaction. It was a peach of a craft to fly. Having made sufficient altitude, he banked steeply and kicked the rudder bar till his compass showed approximately north-north-west. This carried him across the airfield. He was as yet no more than 600 feet up. He recognized the figure of Gregory among the men on the ground. It was, of course, impossible to perceive such things in the circumstances, but Garry had a strong impression that he was grinning.

The Fury climbed swiftly with little labouring of the engine. In a few minutes he began to see the white tops of the Himalayas popping up one after the other beyond the green-clad foothills which screened them at ground level. In another few minutes he could see Kinchinga itself a hundred miles away. He needed no charts for this flight. He had such close acquaintance with Kinchinga that he knew in great detail all the physical aspects of its southern face. Less than half an hour after taking off he was over the mighty peak. He had donned the oxygen mask, for at this height a temporary black-out due to violent movement of the plane with little oxygen in the air was an ever-present possibility. And over such a tumble of high, rugged pinnacles a temporary black-out would probably be fatal.

Garry throttled back until the Fury was only about

20 m.p.h. above stalling speed. He followed the ridge along which he had so laboriously climbed a few days before. Then he let the nose of the machine drop. With distance being so deceptive among the giants it was risky to approach too close to the solid mass. But by following the slope of the mountain towards the glacier valley between the two main ridges, he gave himself space to play with in case of trouble.

With eyes straining against the glare, he sought for the camps. It was a difficult job, for the tents were made of dark material and in most cases were set among equally dark rocks, which thus provided an effective camouflage. He did, however, recognize the dark spot on the eastern slope of the East Ridge which was his own party's now deserted Camp III. He turned and flew upwards along the ridge. In a few minutes he covered what was, on foot, days of heart-breaking toil. He recognized the cliffs where the ridge ended, took in at a glance the route they had taken up the 400-foot cliff, and thus got an idea of the position of Camp IV. Beyond Camp IV was a long, steepening snow slope. From the camp they had seen this slope, like a great whale-backed hummock with the summit of Kinchinga peeping up beyond it. Now, as he looked down on it he could see that beyond the hummock lay yet another bastion, a rocky outcrop flanked by precipitous snow slopes and so steep that he shuddered at the thought of any man attempting to climb it. Maybe a route could be found, but from the air it seemed that at that barrier the expedition must, in any case, have ended.

Still, that was the chance that accompanied any enterprise, Garry reflected. Success was never assured, but unless you tried you most assuredly could not hope to succeed. And the glorious endeavour was perhaps even more important to a man's self-respect and confidence in himself than actual success.

Again Garry rolled the machine over in a steep turn. Then on the snow near the foot of the cliff he had just discovered he saw two black dots. He dived towards them and, at a distance of 400 yards, recognized them as human figures waving to him—Sir Peter and Graham. Apparently they were seeking a route up those spine-chilling cliffs.

Satisfied as to the position there, Garry did a reconnaissance of the basin-like side of the mountain joining the two ridges. Approaching the western ridge, he obtained a view similar to the one he had observed from the East Ridge when, with binoculars, he had witnessed the Americans' crossing of the almost fatal cornice. He could see the gap created by the avalanche quite plainly now. In two minutes he was above the ridge. By keeping his eye on the spot where he had previously seen the camp, he was able to pick it out easily despite the greatly changed contours when he neared it. Then he saw three more figures. They would be Colin, Read, and the Doc. Garry breathed a deep sigh of relief that all three had safely reached the West Ridge. He swooped as low as he dared and could plainly recognize them as men though not as individuals. They waved violently, as though trying to convey some message, but Garry could not comprehend. At any rate they had not succeeded in bridging the gap.

There now remained the real job—that of finding the young Americans. For the first time Garry could appreciate the lie of the land in the vicinity of the West Ridge. The rocks above the gap in the cornice were well broken and seemed to offer little technical difficulty to the experienced climber. Above them was a steep but easily negotiable snow slope which ended once again in appalling cliffs. It looked no go in that direction also. He nosed the plane towards the northern face of the mountain, which was as yet unseen by man. A glance showed that probably the only practicable route to the summit lay to the north, where an extremely steep snow slope flowed unbrokenly from the very top. To get on to the slope it would be necessary to do a long traverse— perhaps 500 or 600 yards—of the cliffs above the West Ridge.

Garry wondered if the Americans had done that. Then he realized that they could not know of the slope on the other side, and without that knowledge the idea of skirting the cliffs was unreasonable. They would not, he conjectured, return to the gap in the cornice, because they knew they could not possibly bridge it. Naturally they could not even guess that by merest chance the mishap had been observed and that Sir Peter's party were attempting rescue. So Garry reasoned that they would seek a way up the forbidding cliffs, hoping for a way out by traversing the summit and descending to the East Ridge. There was no sign of a break in the smooth, glaring white expanse of the summit, so Garry searched the terrain between the cliffs above the cornice and those comprising the last barrier to the summit.

This terrain was much broken up—a jumble of snow, black rocky outcrops and declivities. The rough, broken, and spotted nature of it made recognition of human figures extremely difficult, so tiny would they be in the vast landscape. Garry flew back and forth across the terrain until his tired eyes ached and his head throbbed. It seemed an impossible job. He watched the fuel gauge on the instrument panel anxiously.

It was now four days since the near-fatality. Garry had not the least idea how much food the lads had. Perhaps, being the dare-alls they obviously were, they had decided to risk a flying attack on the summit, carrying only sufficient food for one day. Exposed in such a bitter atmosphere without food for even two days could have a serious effect. Garry began to despair. He glanced at the fuel gauge again, did a rapid calculation, and decided that he could risk, at the outside, another three minutes.

Hardly had he arrived at the decision when he spotted what might be three human figures. He flew low towards them. At two hundred feet, before he pulled the stick back to lift the machine, he could see without any doubt that they were the Americans. They waved to him. He quickly noted prominent landmarks in the vicinity

10

and circled. As he did so he moved the appropriate lever to " Bomb Doors Open " position. Then he ran in again on the course on which he had first seen the lads. They were still there, on a small arête broken by dark, rocky outcrops. On each side of them steep snow slopes swept down to crevasses. Garry realized how almost impossible it would have been to attempt to drop a single package of food. It would have needed to land within a range of fifty feet of the target—a matter of sheer luck with an unstreamlined " bomb," no bomb-aimer, and a speed of over 200 m.p.h.

Garry's thumb rested on the bomb-release button. He swooped towards his target. Judging as near as possible a distance of approximately eighty yards from immediately over the heads of the lads, he pressed the button, praying hard that his makeshift bombs would work. He felt a slight surge in the craft. In two seconds she lifted again. He circled, looking anxiously over his shoulder to see if his plan had worked. Two parachutes floated smoothly earthwards, cans at their bases, and between them stretched a thin dark line.

Garry breathed a sigh of relief. As he flew back across his course he saw the first and lower parachute settle into a deep crevasse. The rope touched earth. Garry could see it sending up little puffs of powdery snow as it dragged. Then the other parachute descended into the gulf on the other side of the arête and the weight of the two cans counter-balanced. As Garry kicked the Fury over to a southwards course he saw the figures moving towards the line. The spider-web principle had worked. Then the figures disappeared beneath his wings.

Ahead lay Milna — and an awful lot of trouble. Officialdom would take a pretty poor view of anyone who pinched an R.A.F. bomber. Nevertheless, as the mountains gradually flattened out towards the plain, Garry removed his oxygen mask and burst into a loud and entirely original rendition of " The Daring Young Man on the Flying Trapeze "—original in that every line was in a different key.

After the first verse he yawned widely. The immediate job had been accomplished ; the Americans had sufficient food and fuel to last at least three weeks, and, although marooned, they were at any rate still safe. So Garry relaxed the physical and mental tension which had gripped him unceasingly for the last four days. He could afford to rest now. He yawned again. His eyelids were heavy and his eyes felt as though they were rimmed with fine sand. It was a tremendous effort to keep awake. The monotonous, steady roar of the engine tended to lull him into drowsiness. But he had to keep awake—just for another quarter of an hour. Once he did doze off, and as his hand weighed unconsciously on the stick the Fury executed such a violent half-barrel roll that it shook him into consciousness. It gave him a bad scare, and he made sure he did not doze off again.

At last the agony of having to keep awake ended. Milna airfield appeared ahead, and he touched down to a perfectly smooth landing. A car raced across the field ahead of a pursuing cloud of red dust. Garry switched off the engine and clambered out of the cockpit. Two R.A.F. police, armed with revolvers, leapt from the car which skidded to a halt. They were followed by Gregory.

" I've got to arrest you, McGowan," Gregory said sternly. Only Garry saw the suggestion of a wink.

" Well, it came off all right," Garry said happily. " The lads won't starve. All they can do now is break their silly necks."

" The stunt worked, then ? "

" Without a hitch."

All four men got into the car. Garry's head, feeling as ponderous as a big melon, rolled on to his chest, his eyes closed, and the jolting of the car rocked him to sleep in a few seconds. The next thing he knew was Gregory shaking him violently. He opened his eyes. His mouth was dry, and the whole world hazy. Automatically he climbed out of the car and accompanied the three men into a building. He was shown into a little white room.

There was a bed of sorts. He stretched himself out on it and was at once asleep.

It was not till fourteen hours later when he awoke, refreshed with a glorious sense of well-being, that he blinked at the dazzling blue sky through a window and noticed that the window was barred. Realization seeped slowly into his sleep-hazy mind. He was in gaol.

CHAPTER IX

THE SUMMIT

An Indian warder opened the iron door. A white official stood behind him.

"The governor wants to see you, Mr. McGowan," said the official.

Garry followed him along a corridor. The official opened a door and stepped aside for Garry to enter. There were three men in the room. He recognized Gregory, who winked covertly. One man wore the uniform of a Group-Captain, the other wore white duck civvies.

"Good morning, McGowan," said the civilian, who was seated at a desk. "I want you to meet Group-Captain Sherringham, whose aeroplane you stole."

Garry was not sure whether he should perform an amiable greeting in his capacity of representative of the *Gazette* or stand stiffly to attention as became a good gaolbird.

"So McGowan of the *Gazette* turns aeroplane thief," boomed Sherringham.

"You weren't there, sir," faltered Garry. "Squadron-Leader Gregory had no authority to lend me a plane, so I—er——"

"So you stole one—fifteen thousand pounds' worth of aircraft."

"I would suggest borrowed as a better expression, sir. I did return it."

" That does not alter the principle. Without authorization you removed an aircraft belonging to His Majesty."

" I'm perfectly willing to pay for damages—if any. I think altogether it came to two parachutes and some petrol. It was a case of necessity. If I didn't get a plane those three lads on Kinchinga would have died. You must realize what a spot they were in and why——"

" You needn't go into details," barked Sherringham. " Gregory has told me the whole story."

" Well, what would you have done if you were me ? " Garry demanded heatedly. " Would you sit down and twiddle your thumbs until officialdom woke itself up ? Those lads would have died before that. What then ? What would *you* have done ? "

" Exactly what you did, McGowan."

Sherringham's stern mask melted and he grinned as he gripped Garry's hand. " I'm glad to know you, McGowan. You put up a darn good show. I know what you did, and it was a wonderful bit of flying. I hope you'll come back and be our guest at lunch at the station."

" Then I'm not a gaolbird any longer ? "

" It's up to me to prefer a charge in these circumstances," explained Sherringham. " I prefer not to."

" You're a sportsman," beamed Garry.

Over lunch Garry gave the officers' mess a pretty detailed report of the expedition's progress, and the change of plan necessitated by the inexperienced American lads getting themselves into trouble.

" They're not out of the wood yet, then ? " asked Sherringham.

" Not by a long chalk," answered Garry. " I have got fuel and food to them. There is enough to last them three or four weeks. That was the first consideration. Without food they would undoubtedly have perished. Now they can last out until we can devise some means of getting them off. At the moment they are marooned. They know they can't bridge the gap where the avalanche occurred and they'll try to find some other way down.

" I took the opportunity yesterday of making a pretty thorough reconnaissance. I don't think anyone has done a recco of Kinchinga from the air. You can see much more from up top than you can when you're actually on the mountain. I'm quite convinced that their only chance is to return to the gap, where three of our fellows have installed themselves, and get across by means of a rope bridge. But they don't know our fellows are there, and I don't imagine they'll go back unless I can let them know the position."

" Why didn't you drop them a message yesterday ? " asked Gregory.

" For two reasons," replied Garry. " In the first place, I was too concerned and too excited to think of anything but getting that grub on to the mountain. In the second place, when I did take off I did not know that Read and Dodd and Meighan had succeeded in negotiating the rim and getting to the cornice."

" How do you propose carrying on from here ? " asked Sherringham.

" Taking Kell's autogyro—which I also stole—back to him, and then slogging up the West Ridge on foot. I'm thinking of trying smoke signals."

" It will take you days to get up there."

" A week at the very least," corrected Garry. " And that would be allowing for the fact that the Americans have pioneered a route and that their camps are still there."

" Could you drop a message by plane ? " asked Sherringham. " I will take the responsibility of lending you a Fury."

" That would be marvellous," said Garry. " But it would be ridiculous using full-size parachutes for a single message. A single parachute would be hopeless. You've got to have lines floating about like spiders' webs to catch on to things. I know what we can do. I'll get a length of cord and make parachutes of small squares of cloth—like the ones kids make from handkerchiefs and weight with stones. Cloth about a yard square and coloured brightly could easily be seen. I'll make seven or eight and attach the message to each one, weight it, and connect them all up by cord so that it must hook them all up somewhere."

" It sounds fantastic," said Sherringham. " But not so fantastic as parachuting oil drums from bomb racks, and somehow or other you managed to do that. Have a crack at it anyway. I'll get some of the fellows busy making the parachutes for you."

That afternoon was a busy one. Sherringham had a plane specially tuned up for the flight. Garry prepared his messages, saw to the manufacture of the parachutes, attached the messages and connected them up with about three hundred yards of strong cord. Then he spent a couple of hours writing up the arrears of his story. The *Gazette* had received nothing since the departure from Camp III nine days before, when the radio had been abandoned for reasons of weight.

The *Gazette* the following morning would have headlines that would transport Carmody into a delirium of delight. Garry could almost see the splash posters and hear the newsboys shouting above the roar of London's traffic : " Climbers Marooned on Himalayan Giant. Dramatic Rescue Efforts."

Soon after sunrise the following morning, basking in the favour of official approval in the person of Group-Captain Sherringham, Garry climbed into a sleek, throatily growling Fury. This time he wore parachute harness. Another minute later and the earth was dropping away from him. He followed the route of two days before and approached the terrain above the cornice gap as he had done on his " bombing raid." He wanted to find the lads first. He noted that the parachute no longer dangled in the crevasse into which he had seen it descend. That meant they had successfully hauled it up, as he had anticipated. But, with engine throttled back as far as he dared, he could not sight them. He circled back and ran in again. Still no sign of them. Each time he came in he flew lower. Increasing confidence in the machine and in himself made Garry bring it dangerously low, skimming along with wing-tips perilously close to beetling crags of ice. It was fool flying, and Garry knew it. But he could not resist the temptation, knowing that the lower he got the more chance he had of spotting the lads.

Then suddenly the plane juttered horribly, the stick whipped violently from his grasp and the icy terrain whirled round him dizzily. A quick glance showed one wing-tip shattered. He fought desperately with the stick and rudder bar, expecting every moment to be blotted out in one tremendous crash. Miraculously the world ceased its mad spinning and he was still alive. But the uneven air pressure on the exterior control surfaces called for considerable physical effort to keep the Fury on an even keel.

When the plane ceased its crazy gyrations Garry saw that he was flying southwards over the great basin. He also realized that he had no chance at all of going back to drop his messages. It was difficult enough to keep the Fury on a level keel as it was, without the necessity for quick and smooth manœuvres. To return would be deliberate suicide.

Bitterly he reflected that he had badly smashed one Fury, that he would be very lucky to land it safely. And he hardly expected Group-Captain Sherringham to hand over another machine, asking him to see what he could do to that one.

Then Garry noted that the Fury was tending to veer to starboard. He applied correction, but immediately it became unmanageable. The controls were so damaged that it was impossible to fly a straight course. It could only keep on an even keel by describing a huge clockwise circle. It had lost a lot of height, too, which in its damaged condition it could not recover. That meant that eventually it would run into a mountain face somewhere.

The situation was critical in the extreme. The only chance Garry had was to bale out. As he looked at the wild, rugged wilderness of ice and snow below him his heart beat more quickly. No man with Garry's zest for living could contemplate a fifty-fifty gamble with death and feel unconcerned about it. Despite the intense cold, sweat broke out on his forehead and his hands grew clammy.

The sharp nose of the Fury veered towards the West Ridge. It was now pointing towards the eminence known as the Little Tower on Barren Kot which had been Kell's vantage-point. Gradually the Tower moved over to port. Garry had about fifteen seconds in which to make up his mind. The West Ridge was the only part of the landscape in the wild orbit of the damaged Fury which could provide him with any chance of establishing contact with the other members of the party—the only human beings in all the vast wilderness. Even so, his chances of baling out and landing on the ridge were very remote. Near where the Little Tower reared up a little to the west of the main ridge there was some semblance of a plateau. He had an area of about two hundred yards square in which he could safely land. But the plane was veering away. Every effort he made to draw it to a straight course brought the helpless feeling of no control.

There was one possibility. If he were upside down the plane would veer in the opposite direction—back towards the Little Tower. Wondering what the manœuvre would do to the crazy plane, Garry took a deep breath and fought hard with the stick. She banked steeply. The horizon slid past the wing-tip and the white mountains appeared above his perspex cowling. The Fury was on its back. Garry succeeded in steadying it there. It was losing height rapidly. He saw the Little Tower swinging towards him. He noted by the snow blowing from its peak that the wind was moderately strong and westerly. He made allowance for that—no mathematical calculation, but an instinctive judgment. Then he thrust back the cowling, removed the oxygen mask, and seized the pin of his safety belt. He waited for it—waited for the small voice of his judgment to whisper : " Now ! "

The wind shrieked through the cowling. Now! He pulled out the pin and kicked hard. The roar of the engine rushed away from him and the icy air whistled through his clothing. His gloved hand fitted into the rip-cord ring. He tugged. There was a faint plop, and he felt a springy pressure from the harness webbing. The parachute ballooned above him. He saw the Fury hurtling downwards, twisting over and over. He saw it strike a wall of ice and rock. There was a great puff of snow like an explosion. The machine became immediately a slow-flying mass of dark fragments floating hundreds of feet in the air. A few seconds later he heard the appalling, shattering crash. The fragments tumbled with seeming slowness into the chasm in an avalanche of streaming snow and licking flame.

Garry looked to see how his judgment had served him. He found he had not been far wrong. Tugging at his parachute strings, he found that he was near enough to the plateau to make it. Two minutes later he was being dragged through thick snow. He worked the quick-release catch and stopped. The parachute, still billowing and controlled by the wind, was swept off the plateau and, flapping idly over the chasm, disappeared from sight.

Garry picked himself up. He had safely transferred from air to land. He thanked his lucky stars for his stratosphere flying suit, which protected him from cold even though its bulk made movement—difficult as it was in the rarefied atmosphere—even more difficult. He guessed the time to be about ten o'clock. That gave him nearly eight hours in which to find food and shelter. Otherwise the outlook would be pretty grim. He surveyed the desolation about him, shading his eyes against the glare. The fact that he had no snow goggles added to his troubles, so that as he plodded along he kept his eyes closed for steps at a time. Snow-blindness really would mean the end.

Before him was the Little Tower, its summit perhaps half a mile away in a direct line. Somewhere up there was Kell's camp. And somewhere below it was the Americans' No. II Camp. He looked along the West Ridge towards Kinchinga's summit. Along that ridge lay their Camp No. III. He decided to climb instead of descending. That would get him nearer to Read, Colin, and the Doc. He could never make Camp No. IV in a day, so he had to be sure of No. III. He started off, keeping in the lee of the ridge.

The hours mounted as he plodded along with laborious slowness. He felt a hollow, gnawing pain in his stomach. As the sun's rays burnt mercilessly, thirst tormented him. He resisted the temptation to relieve the pain by eating snow. With thankfulness he saw the sun move farther down the sky. It seemed to sink towards the horizon with incredible speed. Garry began to feel fear gripping him. In another hour it would be dark. Somewhere on the ridge was the No. III Camp. Somewhere. There was an eminence to his left. He moved towards it and climbed. It was a rock climb on a steep, difficult face. But he had to find some place from which he could survey the lie of the land. It was so difficult, and the physical strain so great, that he was tempted to return and go on along the ridge again.

But he reminded himself that he had never yet turned his back on anything he had set out to do. And he had set out to climb this rock. So on he went until at last he stood panting painfully on the summit. The sun was then only a few degrees above the horizon, and all about lay the interminable sea of mountains. He strained his eyes, seeking anything resembling a camp. There was only the unbroken whiteness of the ridge. Bitterly he turned and gazed back along the route he had come. The Little Tower was now nearly two miles away.

Then suddenly he saw the camp. It lay in a sheltered hollow. He had passed it. And he could never have seen it from his route. He whooped in a dry, cracked voice. When he thought how he had been tempted to turn back from climbing this small peak he shuddered. Had he done so he would have gone forwards into night on the icy mountain and certain death from exposure. He noted the position of the camp, which was about six hundred yards away, and with as much haste as he could muster he descended. The sun had gone down and darkness was rolling quickly over the world as he stumbled the last few yards to the tents. Eagerly he drew back the flap.

There was a soft yellow light inside. A man sat there. He reached for a rifle lying in the corner. Garry leapt on him. For he had seen in that instant that the man was Kell. Then there started a nightmarish struggle. Garry's breath burned like fire in his throat. He gasped for air, conscious only of the writhing strength pitted against him and the dull gleam of a rifle-barrel in the lamplight.

He heard Kell's voice, coming chokingly through his intense physical efforts : " I'll kill you, McGowan. I saw you bale out. I've been waiting for you. You shan't interfere in my affairs again. Your friends will be looking for you. They must have seen you bale out too. But I'm going to kill you. They'll never find you. They'll think you went into a crevasse. And they'll never know I killed you—never."

Garry had been without food, and had been spending his reserves of energy in his efforts during the day. Kell was fresh, and Garry felt his own strength ebbing. Kell got uppermost. Garry tried to thrust him off, but his muscles felt the frustration of trying to push over a brick wall. He felt the dull, painful blows as Kell's fist crashed into his face. The lamplight swam sickeningly as Kell's fingers tightened on his throat.

Then suddenly he could breathe ; the weight had gone. There still seemed to be flailing fists, and he could hear Kell grunting. He could not understand it. His head rang with shrill whistlings, and he could see nothing distinctly—only a vague blur of yellow light. Then he

THE LAMPLIGHT SWAM SICKENINGLY AS KELL'S FINGERS
TIGHTENED ON HIS THROAT.

felt his head being raised. There was the taste of brandy on his lips.

" Are you all right, Garry ? " asked a voice that seemed a thousand miles away.

" Colin," croaked Garry. " Good show." Then he slid swiftly into unconsciousness.

It was not till morning that Garry recovered consciousness. The strain of the previous day, culminating in the scrap with Kell, had run his vitality right out.

" Colin," moaned Garry. " Are you there ? "

" I'm here," said Colin, " and getting some breakfast going."

" Gosh, am I glad you arrived last night ! "

" We were up at the Yanks' No. IV Camp and saw you stooging about in the plane. Then we saw the plane go crazy and you bale out. I left the others and came down to look for you."

" I'm glad you found me when you did."

" So am I, Garry."

" Where's Kell ? "

" In the other tent."

" My face feels as if it's been under a tank."

" It looks a bit that way too. I did touch it up a bit while you were out for the count."

" Thanks."

" What was it all about, Garry ? "

" Kell decided to shoot me the moment he saw my face, that's all. He didn't like my pinching his gyro, and he's still sore about it, I guess."

" I'm certain he's going crazy," Colin said. " I practically had to slug him unconscious, and when I kicked him into the other tent he was babbling like a drunk."

" What about ? "

" The Kinchinga Monster."

" Then he's going crazy all right."

" He wanted to take his gun. Not likely, said I. He nearly wept. Said they were after him—the bogey men, I suppose he meant."

" I want to see Kell," said Garry.

" After breakfast."

" No, now."

" How do you feel ? "

" A bit rocky, but I'll be all right."

Garry crawled out of the tent and into the adjoining one. Kell, who was in a sleeping-bag, sat up with a start. His eyes flashed wide ; they were set in deep hollows ; and they were the eyes of a man who was either mad or in terror of his life.

" All right, Kell," Garry said. " You can relax. I'm not going to beat you up. I just want to get things straight. I don't like you, and I never have. All the same I don't want to see you go berserk. What's on your mind ? Why did you try to kill me ? "

" When I saw the tent flap open I thought it was them," Kell muttered.

" You knew it was me all right when we started scrapping."

" I wanted to kill you, McGowan."

" Why ? "

" Because I hate you. Isn't that a good enough reason ? I'll get you yet, you interfering young swine."

" Cut out talking like a cheap movie picture. Who did you think were coming to get you ? "

" Those plaguey porters. They meant to kill me. I know they did."

" So you've been ill-treating them again, eh ? Well, what do you expect them to do ? "

" They said the Kinchinga Monster was coming and scrammed out of it. They left me alone on the mountain. But it was a trick. They meant to come back and get me. There's no such thing as the Kinchinga Monster, is there ? Is there ? "

" There are some pretty queer things in this world, you know."

" But there can't be."

" Then what are you scared of ? "

" Them. I know there's something on this mountain.

The silence. The queer things you hear in the silence. It's like a haunted house. You never know what the next step will bring."

" Forget all that nonsense about monsters and ghosts and murdering porters, Kell. You've got a bad case of nerves. Come and have breakfast."

Kell struggled out of the sleeping-bag and followed Garry to the other tent. Breakfast was a disturbing meal, with Kell's wild eyes continually flashing from Garry to Colin and back again. Garry told Colin of his flights and his failure to get a message to the marooned lads.

After breakfast Garry discarded his flying overall for a suit of the lighter, specially designed Americans' clothing of which there was a spare kit in the camp. Then, taking provisions, Colin and Garry prepared to depart for No. IV Camp. Garry suddenly remembered Kell's rifle. He picked it up.

" We can't take that," protested Colin. " It's useless weight."

" We can't leave it here with him," said Garry.

" You must leave it with me," whined Kell. " What am I to do ? "

" There's plenty of food, and you're safe enough here. Stay here till we come down."

" You must leave me my rifle. It's my only protection against it—them."

" Oh no," said Garry. " No more chances."

He tossed the rifle from the ridge into the chasm. Kell uttered a hoarse scream. The rifle slithered with increasing speed down the precipitous slope and was lost. Garry and Colin turned and trudged upwards towards Camp No. IV. They arrived about mid-afternoon. The Doc and Read, who had been full of grave misgivings, were overjoyed to see Garry alive and more or less well. He was still a little shaky after the previous night's ordeal.

Over supper that night Garry explained the situation, and it was decided to do a reconnaissance of the gap on the morrow to see what could be done. Early the following morning, before the sun could soften the snow, the three men stood on the cornice surveying the breath-taking gap. Beside them were their rucksacks, filled to capacity.

" If the lads returned to the other side," Garry said, " it would be easy to toss a line across and rig a rope bridge of sorts. But they don't know there's anyone here, and furthermore, they know that the chances of anyone's being here are practically nil, so the possibility of their returning is negligible. They'll be trying to find a way over to the East Ridge, which I know from observation is impossible. The message I wanted to deliver, and failed to, was to tell them to return here."

He looked across to the crags on the other side of the gap.

" You could throw a rope across easily—if there were someone there to catch it," he said.

" Look," said the Doc, pointing. " There's a sharp pinnacle there at a height of about thirty feet. Remember that time you got us out of trouble in North Wales ? Could you repeat the trick and lasso it ? "

Garry looked at the rock in silence for a long time. Then he took a length of line, removed a glove and made a running noose. The bitter cold was like fire to his fingers. He fumbled the noose quickly and donned his glove, swinging his arm and waggling his fingers to get the blood circulating again. The danger from frostbite was considerable. He measured the distance to the crag with his eye. By any standard it was a good long throw. Here, encumbered by clothes and the limit to exertion imposed by the lack of oxygen, it was a task indeed. He coiled the lariat and swung the noose above his head. Then with a tremendous effort he let it fly. It snaked through the air. It went to one side of the crag and in any case it dropped before it made the distance. Garry sank into the snow, gasping for breath. The effort had taken as much out of him as a hardly con-tested mile race. He waited for a quarter of an hour, until his heart had stopped racing and was again pulsing normally. Then he tried again. This time the noose settled over the crag.

The others cheered loudly as Garry lay panting in the snow. While Garry recovered his breath, the others drove several pitons, or iron spikes equipped with metal rings, deep into the hard snow.

Having recovered his breath, Garry tested the rope with which he had lassoed the crag. It was quite firm. Colin attached a rope to his own waist while he made a turn of the lariat round his chest and a loop at the end into which he put one foot. Then he swung himself into the space over the fearful gap. Colin gently eased the rope that passed from his hands to the pitons and back to his waist. Were it not for the controlling rope he would be killed by the force with which he would swing against the rocks opposite. At last he got safely across and disengaged himself. The rope was pulled back to the other side of the gap and Garry followed in like manner. Then came the Doc and lastly Read. With the last man across a sort of rope bridge remained, as the control rope passed from the crags, across the gap, through the pitons, and back to the crags. On the return journey the first man across would suspend his weight on the lariat while the other three would haul on the control rope, one end of which would be attached to his waist. The pitons would act more or less as pulleys and the man would be drawn to the other side of the gap.

Having made the ropes of the " bridge " secure, the four men roped up and commenced the moderate climb up the cliffs. They reached the broad terrain on which Garry had seen the lads from the plane two days before. Their position would be roughly a mile from where the Englishmen reached the plateau. All four men indulged in considerable shouting but got no reply. Garry led his companions towards the place where he had seen the lads. They found the rope he had attached to the cans. They followed it in both directions and found the parachutes. One can was there—empty. The other can had been detached.

Obviously they could not attempt to carry an awkward and bulky can about with them. Therefore they must have put it in some cache, where, if they ran short of food, they could easily find it. There was nothing else the Englishmen could do that night, so they picked out what they judged to be the most sheltered spot and made for it. There they found the missing can unbroached. It was, they realized, the obvious place for the Americans to have put it. Garry and his companions pitched bivouac camp for the night.

In the morning Garry was seized by a brilliant idea. He had had no time to clean out the oil drums before delivering them. The contents of the drums were in tins anyway and so could not be affected. But in packing the drums he had used newspaper stuffing to keep the contents firm and thus render the " bombs " less liable to bursting in the event of a hard landing. He gathered all the paper packing from the empty can, returned to the bivouac camp, opened the other can, and removed all the oil-impregnated paper from that one too. He screwed the paper up well, poured the dregs of thick, viscous oil on it, and set it alight. A tent fabric made a satisfactory damper. By alternately covering and uncovering the burning stuff, dense black puffs of smoke rose lazily in series in the clear air, Red Indian fashion. There was nothing else that could be burned, everything else being a necessity. The party decided to do nothing that day, but to wait and see what effect the signals might have.

The idea worked. Late that afternoon three figures staggered across the snow to the bivouac. Never were men more pleased to see men. There was an absolute orgy of hand-pumping and back-slapping. Over the simple supper that was as exciting as a banquet, yarns were exchanged and future plans discussed. The boys had been trying to find a route but had everywhere met sheer, unclimbable walls of rock or ice.

Regretfully the conclusion was reached that Kinchinga

had won. There had been so much time lost, so much of the precious stores laboriously carried high on the mountain used in rescue efforts. And soon the weather would break and render any attempt on the mountain impossible for a whole season. The morrow must mean a return. Read and the Doc would accompany the Americans, and Garry and Colin would do the traverse to the East Ridge to inform Sir Peter and Graham of developments, and then return with them.

The following morning the seven men stood on the edge of the terrain preparatory to descending the cliff to the gap. Garry walked to the edge and looked down towards the gap. What he saw made him gasp. The rope stretching from the pitons to the cliff was no longer there. A few feet, still attached to the pitons, lay on the snow. And standing there was Kell. Garry shouted. Kell pointed towards him and laughed. The laughter floated up thinly. It was the laughter of a maniac. Kell turned and staggered back down the ridge, his idiotic laughter fading as he went.

"He's gone stark crazy," muttered Garry. "He's been ill-treating the porters and got an idea they meant to get him. Either they or the Monster. That idea and the silence and loneliness of the mountain have shaken him clean off his rocker."

Garry looked at the faces of his companions. They showed despair. All seven of them were now marooned. Food which would last for three weeks for three men would last less than half that time for seven. It was a seemingly hopeless position. Sir Peter and Graham could have no idea of what had taken place, and having been unsuccessful in reaching the summit from the East Ridge would probably be waiting at Camp IV as long as possible in case the American lads managed to do a traverse with the idea of descending by the East Ridge.

"We're sunk," said Colin shakily.

"Not while there's life," said Garry. "We've got one chance. We can only save our skins by climbing Kinchinga itself."

" It can't be done," said Larry Elmer. " We've been trying to find a route for days."

" When I did that first recco flight," said Garry, " I got a pretty good idea of the landscape thereabouts. From the air there is apparently nothing but cliffs and impossibly steep snow slopes between the ridges. But there is one route that might go. That is from the north."

" But how do we get to the north ? " asked Tex. " We're trapped."

" If we can do a traverse of the cliffs on the extreme left of this ridge we can make it."

" Those cliffs are exposed," protested Larry Elmer. " I wouldn't like to try to climb round them at three thousand feet, let alone twenty-two thousand. You'd be frozen solid before you got fifty yards."

" Well, we've got to try it," said Garry, shrugging his shoulders. " It's our only chance."

The party decided to investigate. They returned to the site of the bivouac camp and packed into their rucksacks every bit of food they could possibly carry. All day long they tramped laboriously over the badly broken terrain with its treacherous crevasses. Twice snow that was seemingly solid crumbled, and members fell into the ice-walled depths of unsuspected crevasses. But roping and careful movement prevented tragedy. At nightfall they pitched the bivouac tents in a sheltered place and the following morning pushed on again. At last they reached the place where the terrain ended and fell away precipitously. Only the cliffs of rock and ice continued, their walls rising sheer for nearly a mile.

" Well, this is it, McGowan," said the Doc grimly. " What about it ? "

Garry looked at the seemingly impossible cliffs.

" We don't have to climb up," he said. " We climb along."

Colin, his eyes screwed up, was surveying the cliffs.

" I might make it—in decent weather, that is ; not this half-gale."

The other six looked at him with new hope in their eyes. It was not for nothing that Sir Peter had asked Colin to join the expedition. He was one of the most brilliant of the younger rock-climbers in England. But his attempt on these cliffs would be no sporting attempt. It would be a desperate climb for life, demanding every atom of energy and technical skill.

In the afternoon the gale stiffened, moaning and screaming through the crags. Snow fell in increasing volume. The party was driven to seek shelter. For three days the storm raged, while the seven men remained in the tiny bivouac tents with nothing to do but eat—sparingly—and talk and listen to the ghostly howling of the wind, wondering how long the storm would last while their limited rations ebbed away.

Then on the fourth day the storm abated considerably. The party edged towards the cliffs. Colin surveyed them with experienced eye.

" It's now or never," he said.

" It's madness," muttered the Doc.

" Well, it's all up with us if we stay anyway, isn't it ? " demanded Colin. " I can see one route that might go. I want two of you to come with me and try it."

Garry and Larry Elmer raised their hands. The three young men roped up. Colin started along a perilous ledge. Garry didn't like the look of the exposed face, but he knew it was take the chance or die. Colin was undoubtedly a brilliant climber. He seemed to have the same adhesive power on the rock as a fly on a ceiling. He moved by short pitches, expertly singling out the most likely routes and climbing with perfect balance and rhythm. He coached the others, who moved one at a time. While one man moved, the other two managed the rope.

On the exposed cliff and puffing heavily in the thin air, with an icy wind penetrating allegedly wind-proof clothes, they suffered torture that it seemed must never end. But at last they reached a broad ledge, and it was apparent that the snow slope could then be reached by easy, well-broken rocks. The three then returned in the same slow, painful manner. It was well into the afternoon when they arrived back to the camp to report.

On the following morning the weather still remained moderate and the great traverse began. Colin's skill alone nursed the party across the cliff face. Without his leadership the venture would surely have ended in disaster. The seven men, moving one at a time, made exasperatingly slow progress. No meal could be eaten on such ledges, where hand-holds were a constant necessity. Hands were constantly steadying foot-holds or groping for clefts. Soon after five in the afternoon the whole party had reached the snow on the other side of the cliffs. They were exhausted, ashen-faced, and aching terribly from bitter cold and hunger. But the traverse had been accomplished and they looked towards the steep snowy slope of Kinchinga with hope in their hearts.

A hot meal was prepared and the bivouac tents pitched. Never had men settled so eagerly into the comparative warmth of their sleeping-bags. The following morning a reconnaissance showed that Kinchinga could be skirted on snow all the way, which would bring the party to the cliffs that had baffled Sir Peter and Graham. But they would be *above* the East Ridge, and by ropes and purchases could *descend* where the other two could not *ascend*.

The seven men, now well fed and rested, decided to move early. The weather was unusually still. And there lay Kinchinga—unconquered. Colin looked towards it.

" I believe we could do it," he said. " We could go up and over and down the other side."

The men looked at each other in conjecture.

" It's not done for seven men to climb a Himalayan giant," said the Doc. " It makes it look too easy. It's usual for one or two only to reach the summit—if ever they do."

" Then why not attempt a precedent ? " asked Garry.

And so it was decided. The party moved off, climbing in snow. Night brought them to within eight hundred feet of the summit. It had been an uneventful, even a dull climb. A few steep sections called for some step-cutting and that was all. Nevertheless it had been strenuous work, the lack of oxygen at this, the highest level they had achieved, rendering it necessary to breathe deeply twice for every step taken.

The next morning they set off again, and within two hours were fifty yards from the flat plateau of the summit. Colin was leading the roped party. He halted for a moment.

" It's in the bag, boys," he said.

" And somehow it isn't very exciting," Garry added. " It's been so darned easy after the cliff face that it's almost anti-climax."

Colin made to move on. Garry took his arm and held him back.

" Who is going to be first on Kinchinga ? " he asked. " Britain or America ? "

" I guess it's Colin's party-day," said Larry Elmer. " If he hadn't got us around the cliff I guess we'd never have got anywhere—except maybe the next world."

" If you hadn't been so deuced game as greenhorns and bought yourself this packet of trouble we'd never have got *our*selves into trouble, too. And if we hadn't got into trouble we'd never have got here either," retorted Colin.

" If Garry hadn't bombed us we wouldn't have had the grub to carry on," Ted reminded them.

" All right," said Garry. " This will settle it." Groping under his clumsy clothes he produced the penny which once before had settled a point of contention. He tossed it.

" Heads," called Colin.

" Tails," announced Garry and hastily pocketed the coin. " America wins."

Larry Elmer and his two friends took the lead, and a few minutes later had the honour of being the first men ever to stand on Kinchinga's summit. The others were with them in a few moments. They stood silently gazing at the incredible tumble of gigantic snow-covered mountains.

" Well, this is it, chaps," murmured the Doc.

" One more great mountain conquered," said Garry. " This seems pretty tame now, but we've made mountaineering history."

" Yep," agreed Larry. " I guess we have."

There was suddenly an orgy of hand-shaking. But no one cheered. Somehow there was a faint feeling of disappointment that they had destroyed something which had become almost a legend—the invincibility of Kinchinga.

They stayed on the summit for an hour, then reluctantly turned and trailed down the slope towards the East Ridge.

ENVOI

THE descent was uneventful. Except for the breath-taking descent of the cliffs above the East Ridge, which was accomplished with the aid of ropes, it was little more than a long, laboured, tiring walk. The party, having picked up Sir Peter and Graham *en route*, descended by their old route on the East Ridge. At the Base Camp they found the Sherpas waiting, and were glad to be relieved of a considerable part of their load.

Then the expedition crossed to the alp above the Banghiri Gorge to acquaint Green of the story and take him back with them to civilization. They expected to find Kell there too. But he had not returned to the camp on the alp.

" The Kinchinga Monster got him," said Green. He thumbed over his shoulder in the direction of one of the American party's porters. Garry recognized the man as the one he and Colin had seen sitting sullenly apart on the occasion of their visit to the American party just below the waterfall. It was the man Kell had thrashed.

Green called the fellow over and spoke to him in his native dialect. None of the others understood the conversation.

" He says the Monster took Kell and carried him off high up on the mountain," said Green.

" Ask him what the Monster looked like," said Garry.

Another conversation ensued.

" He says he was too afraid to look," announced Green.

Garry looked at the impassive oriental face, and decided the matter was best left alone. If Kell had been alive he would have had to face a charge of attempted murder anyway.

Sir Peter was speaking over dinner the same night : " Mind you, I hardly consider the conquering of Kinchinga a true mountaineering feat. It was only the extra food that you dropped on the mountain, McGowan, that made it possible. As a purist in mountaineering matters I disapprove of such methods."

" I'm only sorry, sir," said Garry, " that circumstances precluded your getting to the summit yourself."

" Graham and I are not disappointed," retorted Sir Peter. " We can take defeat like sportsmen and gentlemen—if there is any difference in the terms. We are, as a matter of fact, already planning another expedition to climb Kinchinga."

" But Kinchinga has already been won," said Garry.

" That means nothing. I don't care if every Cook's tourist in India goes up it in an arm-chair in a funicular railway, I am determined to climb it myself on my own two feet. You wouldn't care to join us, McGowan ? You've proved yourself a useful man on a mountain."

" Not on your life," laughed Garry. " Once is quite enough for me."

Garry excused himself, rose and betook himself to finish tapping out on the radio one of the biggest stories of his career. He chuckled as he imagined the expression that would mould Carmody's face when he got the cable announcing the safe return of both parties and the successful joint Anglo-American assault on Kinchinga, Queen of the Himalayas.